RANDOM FACTOR

PULP FACTION>PO BOX 12171>LONDON>N19 3HB
http://www.pulpfact.demon.co.uk

Editor: Elaine Palmer
Assistant Editor: Robyn Conway
Cover design: Engine
Designers: Michael Kowalski, Joanna Hill.
Original Artwork: Amanda Gazidis, Mark Dove
Distributors UK: Central Books 0181 986 4854
Website: http://www.pulpfact.demon.co.uk
Thanks to: London Arts Board, the Arts Council,
and to all the writers and artists who
have contributed to Pulp Faction.

Contents

B lur bs

I got my first Blurb™ when I was
only five images old. Mummy
Wave bought it for me, a present
for my first ever press
conference. Oh, she was so
proud! Her only daughter, the
youngest girl in the street to
achieve a press-con.

Imagine the headlines.
The in-depth analysis:

*YOUNG GIRL WITNESSES VICIOUS
MURDER! ANGRY MOTHER
DEMANDS PUBLIC RECOGNITION
FOR GRIEVING CHILD. NEW VIRUS
INFECTS GAMEWORLD™!
AUTHORITIES AT LOSS TO EXPLAIN
KILLING.*

Jeff Noon

Media Virgin

Tommy Smart was my best ever friend, and I miss his tactics dearly. We were playing Corporate Sleazeball™ on the Game-Pimp™. Tommy was so good, he'd already scored seven freebies, five perks, four liquid lunches and two complete take-overs against me, easy pickings, before the bad thing happened. At first it was just a whirling shadow at the very edge of my game-vision, a mild intrusion from reality, nothing to be scared about. Perhaps our collected Mummies were calling to us, to come eat?

Before I knew quite what was happening, the shadow-shape had pounced on Tommy, hard and fast. It splintered his game-play into a million pieces and then sucked his image clean away. I pulled out of the Pimp, double-quick and falling...

Into my mother's arms. Back to the Real World™, as Tommy's image drained away to zero before my startled eyes.

Marketing disaster!

Zero-image was a kind of slow death. Tommy didn't really die, he just became a nobody, which was classed as murder one in those days. I couldn't bear to play with him now that he had no flaunt, no flourish, no publicity-value. I guess his erasure made me too famous, far too quickly. Whatever, the Comcops™ soon came knocking, and I was hauled off to give the press-con. I had to give this tear-stricken speech about what a noble player Tommy Smart had been. The newshounds asked me a ton of questions about the monstrous virus that had wiped Tommy's image off the map. I said it was a twisting whirl of data-smoke, dark and brutal, like a tornado, only more fashionable. I was already learning how to work the media.

The next morning's editions were full of artists' impressions of the Twister Wipe™ virus, and how it would kill all the game-pimping children unless caught quickly. Thus was my fifth image-change achieved.

Grieving Witness

From "Media Virgin" to "Grieving Witness",
all in one easy move.

Mummy Wave was so pleased with my
press-con that she bought me the pet as a
reward for being so open to notoriety. Blurb
Worms were rare and expensive in those days,
but Mummy had sold my story to one of the
more down-market newshounds. A girl of
just five images old, imagine, already the
proud owner of an Autovert™, a symbiotic
promo machine.

I called him Scoop™.

Scoop was only three inches long to start with,
and a pale cream colour. I kept him safe and warm
in a glass tank filled with earth and sawdust.
Following the instructions in the user's manual,
Scoop's first meal consisted of five metazine
articles about my witnessing the Evil Twister
at play, a mating pair of Vids reproducing my
press-con, and the complete series of
howlings my mother's exclusive had produced
from the newshound.

Mummy Wave threw a party to celebrate
my exploits, inviting all of the street's
residents. I allowed Scoop out of his tank for
the first time. By now the blurb had
completely swallowed my hot news story. He'd
grown an inch in size with the info, and his
once-naked body now sported the colours of
my new brand image, my very own logo.
Tina Wave Enterprises™, ran the letters along
his spine. The Blurb Worm sat lovingly on my
shoulder, beaming his messages of goodwill...

IMPORTANT PRESS RELEASE! TINA WAVE IS CURRENTLY RECOVERING FROM HER TRAUMATIC EXPERIENCE AT THE HANDS OF THE TWISTER WIPE. SHE WILL NOT BE PERFORMING FURTHER INTERVIEWS UNTIL AFTER THE PUBLICATION OF VOLUME ONE OF HER MEMOIRS.

That was my name, in those days: Tina Wave. It was short for Christina Waverly. Just like *Blurb* was short for Bio-Logical-Ultra-Robotic-Broadcaster. In other words, an Autovert. Just like the Comcops were really the Communication Police. It was the Golden Age of Appearances™. We didn't even call them *names* back then; rather we had logos, or corporate identities, or else brands or trademarks, copyrighted designs, slogans, tags or communiqués.

Nothing was real, and that's how we liked it.

Meanwhile, more and more kiddie players were twisted to zero-image. The Wipeout rampant. The Comcops could only patrol the games, like the useless watchdogs that they were, discovering zero, zero everywhere.

Scoop™

My sixth image was "Lone Vixen". I retired to my bedroom, and stayed there a whole season, writing my memoirs and formulating my game-plan for the public-life ahead. Scoop also went into hibernation, enfolding himself in a cocoon of secreted commercials. Everything slowed down; kids worldwide were absent from the Game-Pimp machine, called off by horror-struck parents. Of course, most kids really wanted to have a go against the Twister, relishing the image they would gain by killing him. But parental advice prevailed, and the Big Pimp's profits fell almost to zero.

Sometimes Tommy Smart came round to see me, but my mother never let him inside the house. I would watch from my upstairs window; his thin, weak, almost transparent body disappearing into the afterglow. But what could I do? After all, he had no commercial value.

By my seventh image-change I had acquired another five Blurbs, including a rather lovely female specimen I called Gossip Monger™. My latest image was "Petulant Brat", and the Blurbs actively promoted that labelling throughout the street. Scoop had meanwhile outgrown his wormhood; he emerged triumphant from his shell, his new wings fluttering madly to dry themselves. Two hours later he was airborne. Scoop became a Flyer™, reproducing my image joyfully over the entire village.

PRESS RELEASE!
TINA WAVE IS NOW
OPEN FOR BUSINESS.
READ HER MEMOIRS.
LET HER MANAGE
YOUR CAMPAIGN.
BECOME AS FAMOUS
AS SHE IS!

By the time I was ten images old ("Crazy Alien Kid on Planet Earth by Mistake!") I had a hundred or so Blurbs flying around the whole city, and a hundred more waiting to hatch their messages from cocoons. Mummy Wave didn't need to buy the worms anymore. Following Scoop's courtship and mating with Gossip (and the birth of the first of their larvae, Blabbermouth™) the other Blurbs were soon hard at it, making their own babies. But Scoop was the official King of Blurbs™, and I was the Queen of Publicity™. The famous Tina Wave, the young girl behind the release of winged logos. I should have realised the problem: I was becoming famous for being *famous*, not for actually perpetrating any new major stories. I was making a handsome profit from my marketing business, thank you, but nothing stupendous had happened to me in the last few years. I was becoming a media-ghost, fed by past glories only.

I really should have realised.

Image number thirteen: "Sullen Bitch-Goddess". I reached puberty. My images had now started to outstrip my years. I had a thousand or so Blurb Flyers surrounding my body by then, thanks to Mummy's desperate attempts to over-extend my public-life. She had started to feed the Blurbs with Junk Mail™, a nasty subscription-hormone that made the Autoverts go sex-mad. They birthed a buzzing halo-wave of publicity. They worked as one, this new swarm of logos, arranging their bodies into a collective display. Hanging over the city like a cloud of desire.

Blurb Flyer

PRESS RELEASE! BUY TINA WAVE'S LATEST OUTPUT! VOLUME TWO OF HER MEMOIRS, NOW OUT! LEARN THE SECRETS OF HER PUBLICITY DRIVE!

It seemed that the whole world must know about my exploits; but really, it was only publicity about publicity. Self-replication of the Image, which is a kind of inbreeding. The Blurb Worm user's manual was very strict on this point: "Lack of cross-pollination can lead to mutant images." You bet! My fourteenth image was "Psychotic Juvenile!" My fifteenth: "Teenage Nympho." And the Blurbs were becoming ever more hungry: "Info! More info!" they buzzed in ragged formation. "Feed us! Feed us major stories!"

Myself and my images were becoming clichéd and malformed, thanks to the limited meme-pool. "Do something, Tina!" cried Mummy Wave from her sunken armchair. She was slowly dying from lack of reflected fame.

Shrinking.

Even the Twister Wipe seemed to have chosen retirement, having by now claimed its forty-seventh victim. The games went easy, safe and boring.

By that time, a lot of the other kids had Blurbs of their own (as the worms became cheaper in price) and the pitched battles between various publicity campaigns left the streets covered in media-corpses. The Comcops charged in too late to erase the débâcle, and my poor army suffered terrible losses in the Blurb Wars. I found dear old Scoop and Gossip lying dead in the street, and their firstborn son, Blabbermouth, crying all over the remains. I buried the two warriors in a grave of obituary columns.

HERE LIE SCOOP AND GOSSIP. LONG MAY THEY PROPAGATE.

Six weeks of fragile peace, with Mummy Wave on her last breaths: "Do something drastic and stupendous, Tina!" Her final press release, giving in to the zero-image: "Save the family's brand-identity! Save the logo!"

Mummy met her deadline. So sad.

A day later I heard from a disgruntled newshound that Tommy Smart's body had been found. Apparently he had killed himself, hanging his emptiness from a streetlamp. One final streetvert, his second death. The roguehound hadn't been allowed to cover the story; as far as the Editors™ were concerned, Tommy was already dead.

No life beyond the image.

The Blurb Wars, the deaths of Scoop and Gossip and Mummy Wave, the disappearance of the Twister: these events all raised my public profile slightly. I came to realise that Death was the ultimate advertisement. This got me to thinking about how Tommy Smart's demise had fuelled my first real image. Gathering my remaining Flyers about me, I ventured into the old entertainment. Corporate Sleazeball.

Oh, such a sad afterglow of its former fame, the game; peopled by just a few rules, just a few lonely players. One such was a young boy of a mere five images, playing "Lone Wolf" against the Corporation UK. I ordered my Blurbs into a whirlwind of darkness, reconstructing my peripheral vision of the Twister Wipe. How easy it was, to replicate the whirlwind! We descended, hard and fast. Blabbermouth led the attack, the newly crowned King of Blurbs. We wiped that boy! Did we? We spun that lonely boy into zero. We just had to do it, you understand, to feed the mouthpiece.

I made my claim; that the Twister Wipe had once again struck, and that I was, once again, the "Grieving Witness" to his crimes.

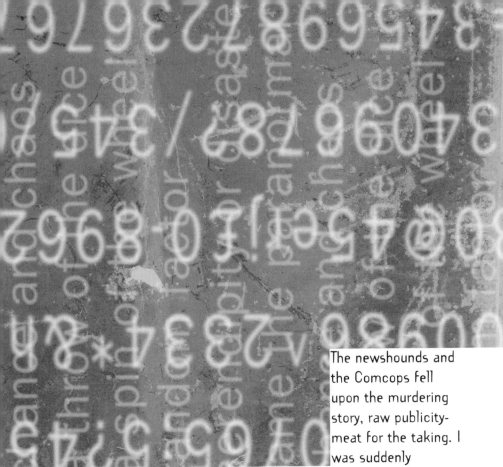

The newshounds and the Comcops fell upon the murdering story, raw publicity-meat for the taking. I was suddenly smothered in Flyers, as they fed upon my fresh notoriety. I was being eaten by fame. The whole city of rival Blurbs had to bow down to my brilliant comeback. My sweet photo-opportunity. A photoworm tried to rape me with his zoom lens. Blabbermouth turned that puparazzo inside-out.

I was liquid from the pulled-off crime. King Blabber fed his campaigns direct to my brain. Did we sizzle! He fertilised the eggs of the lovely, lonely Tina Wave. Our marriage was the talk of the town, and my eighteenth image became "Teenage Mummy", as our baby daughter was born in a blaze of publicity. This was the first time an Autovert had mated with a human, and the newshounds were ravenous. I named the resultant baby Ballyhoo Gosh™, a child of the soft sell.

Seasons go by, with me wishing for nothing more, only that my child should be free from image-pain. Ballyhoo was a beautiful human girl, ridden with subliminal ads. She was hooked on game-pimping. Sometimes I followed her, just to make sure she was Playing Safe™, you understand. No more than that.

Tina Wave

The Big Pimp™ had made a new game, guaranteed free from all adverts and monsters. Often would I watch my daughter making deep-game with strangers. Because the world was turning away from the image, finally. Image Overload™, the experts called it: that moment of evolution where an audience tires of a campaign. My loving Blurbs were dying, one by one, shrivelling into forgotten stories. Falling to zero. Blabbermouth, my husband, my creation, last ever living friend, only survivor. I was becoming a failed publicity campaign.

Days so lazy.

One time I heard my daughter calling, all the way from Gameworld. I slipped into the latest game, searching. A ravenous twirl of shadows come to swallow her whole. The Twister Wipe was back, only older, weaker, more slow. In the whirlwind I saw countless children cry, Tommy Smart among them. The virus had eaten all the images, all the knowledge.

There was a screaming face amid the tornado, almost unrecognisable. It swooped on Ballyhoo Gosh, hungry for info. Bally was fighting back with damage-limitation ads and product-recalls. I came in strong, flying, riding old Blabbermouth like the golden warrior he once was, to our daughter's rescue.

Joined in battle, the three of us wounded the Twister. It spiralled down to a slow wave of fear. One last whirl caught Blabbermouth off guard. He fell to the gameboard, dragging me with him.

Ballyhoo was crying over the body of the Twister: "Grandmama!" she was screaming, "Grandmama!" She had recognised the image, beyond the first death. I walked over to the scene, where Mummy Wave's final image was being zeroed. "Tina Brand," she whispered, "I just had to do it, don't you see? I had to kill Tommy Smart, and all the others. Didn't you have to do the same? To make yourself famous. Can't you see the need!"

Games fall away: I was killing my own mother.

Welcome To The Working World

by Vicky Grut

Nutters – the world is full of
them.

I'm walking in the park with
Jackie at the weekend and I say,
'Jackie, am I dreaming or is there
a dog up in that tree?'

She's laughing. And we stop
and watch this great fat black
dog lumbering from one branch
to another up in this oak tree.
There's a woman with a wide
mouth and a spreading waist
standing at the bottom of it,
clapping her hands and calling:
'Good boy! Clever boy!'

Then she holds out her arms
and the dog drops straight out of
the tree into them.

'Do that often, does he?' I say
to the woman when they come
past us on the path. She's
laughing too.

'Oh yes,' she says, 'I lift him
up and he's away. There's
nothing to beat climbing trees.
Some days I join him. You've got
to have some compensation for
being over forty!'

'Right,' I say.

We stand there watching as
they chase off across the

common together, the woman and the dog: two shapeless, happy nutters. And I say to Jackie, 'Any longer in this job of mine and I'll be climbing trees, never mind waiting till I'm forty.'

*   *   *   *   *

Then it's Saturday and we're off to the States. Tony's got Marco supporting the Blazing Ashcans on their ten state tour (campuses mainly). Back in the office, people are confident because we've just released his 12-inch single and it's selling well over there. The Yanks, apparently, think he's very deep. We have to get there first, though.

I go to Marco's house nice and early. We're supposed to be in the taxi by three, at the airport by four-thirty, on the plane by seven; so I get to Marco's place for one o'clock, but even this isn't early enough. Marco is sitting in the corner of the front room, staring at the tank of tropical fish. The place is a tip. Nothing is packed. Andy, who is supposed to make sure this kind of thing doesn't happen, sits watching re-runs of Captain Scarlet on video: 'Oho, the Mysterons!' says he. 'Watch your back Captain!'

'What do you two jokers think you're doing?' I say, trying to keep it light. I don't want to let them see how much I'm panicking. Inside I'm all jelly.

'I'm not going,' says Marco. He looks at me with his sharp little baby face and his sea-blue eyes. He looks back at the fish again.

I pretend to find this funny. 'Nice one, Marco.'

'I'm serious,' he says. 'I really don't feel like doing anything at all, Steve. I think I'll just have a quiet day today.'

When I was a kid I used to think work was something clear-cut and different to what you did at home. But now I know that it's just about who you're doing things for and why. Like me minding

Marco. You have to do everything for him: buying clothes, shoes, getting his hair cut (I get Jackie to take him shopping, usually), making sure he gets to places on time – these are things most people do for themselves for free but, because you can't trust Marco with the simplest thing, it becomes part of my job.

'You're booked on a transatlantic flight in a couple of hours time whether you feel like it or not,' I say to him now. 'You have a schedule, Marco. You have a contract. You have a commitment to the Blazing Ashcan lads. Remember?'

'Oh Steve,' Marco sighs, 'get them to change the ticket to tomorrow. I'll probably feel better tomorrow. Tell them I'm coming down with something.'

I stop for a minute. I could do this. Yes. Certainly. I can see that the life seems to have gone right out of him today and I am worried. But it's not exactly a reason to change our plans. In fact, it's a good reason to go ahead. I have this uncomfortable feeling that if I don't get Marco on the plane today there will be no end to the things unravelling and falling by the wayside.

I used to be a bit more casual about schedules when I first started. I'd think, well these people have difficult lives, maybe they need a bit of flexibility, they're artists after all. But I've learned that it's fatal to relax your grip. You have to make them see that rules are for sticking to. Forget art if you can't keep up with the routine. They're working for the record company, after all, just like me. That's my attitude. That's my job. (PR man? I'm nothing but a glorified baby-minder, I say to Jackie sometimes.)

I get on the mobile to Jackie. She's out. Where I have no idea (she didn't mention having anything to do today), but I leave a message for her to meet us at the airport in two hours. 'Urgent,' I say. 'I can see I'm going to need some back-up here.'

I can imagine her saying, 'I don't get paid for this you know,

Steve!' But I know she will be there if she can.

'Watch this bit, this bit is great,' says Andy, punching up the volume on the tv. 'Captain Scarlet to the rescue again! Look out you creeps! Take that! POW! Brilliant!'

It's one twenty: time to start picking up speed.

'Andy, a word in the kitchen,' I say, really short and snappy.

'Wow!' says Andy. 'Straight into the fuselage; out with the bomb! But where's the timer? Uh-oh!'

'Andy?' I say, shades of warning in my voice. He gets up and follows me into the kitchen like a lamb.

A lot of it is about confidence. If you act as if you know what you're doing, chances are that people will want to believe you do. You hear these stories of car mechanics who decide to become doctors: they read a couple of copies of *The Lancet* and put on a white coat and suddenly people are letting them deliver babies and diagnose cancer. Nobody really wants to believe that a person can't do their job. Because, of course, when you start to question it you see that most people can't, even if they aren't technically frauds. I say to Jackie sometimes: Look at all these people in responsible positions all over the country – dumping toxic waste in rivers, stuffing food with additives, getting poor ignorant sods to sign up for time-share apartments in Spain, selling legally poisoned meat – they are all just doing their jobs. They are not to blame for the unfortunate side effects of their efficiency and enthusiasm. You can't be expected to sit and think about the consequences of every little action. You think about your job and what you need to do to get your job done; anything more and you go crazy.

And anyway, people don't want to know. I've been trying to tell them back at the office for months now that there's something seriously wrong with Marco. I said it to Tony when he was planning the tour. I said: sit down and talk to him, Tony, see for yourself. Of course when Tony came round, Marco was as sane as you or me; very pleasant, rattling on about the new songs he was writing and not a word about his mother appearing on News at Ten or the people following him everywhere in small black cars. Afterwards Tony said to me, 'If you think you're not up to this, Steve, if you're at all worried about handling this tour, just say. I can give it someone else. No pressure.' I knew what he meant. I can speak Veiled Threat as well as the next person.

Standing in the kitchen with Andy I start to sweat just thinking about all this. I'm on my own, not even Jackie here to help right now. For a minute I wonder where she might be. I know she's not working today.

Back in the other room, Marco is leaning against the tank, staring into the eye of a very slow, yellow fish. He shows no interest in Andy or me. I feel sorry for him. He looks small and slightly lost. He seems to attract the maternal types but none of them stay very long. He doesn't even have his own band for company anymore. It's mostly backing tapes and film projection and lights. A couple of soul singers and a sax player come on half way through his set and there's a fire-eater at the end, but it's not the same as having a band. They come and go. They all do other work. I wouldn't like his life.

I go back to the kitchen and close the door behind me. 'Did he sleep last night?' I say to Andy.

'Not a lot I don't think,' said Andy. He's shamefaced now he's away from the TV. He knows he should have called me earlier. 'Bit of a bad sign isn't it?'

Andy and Marco are friends from way back; I think they may even have gone to school together. He played drums in Marco's first band. He's nothing to do with the music side any more. He just orders the odd taxi, Indian take-aways, pizzas. If you ask him he'll say he's Marco's personal manager. I think he's useless but Marco likes to have him around.

'Look, we've got to get him on that plane,' I say. 'Once he's there he may snap out of whatever this is. Or we find him a psychiatrist or something. But if he stays in this house another day he will never make the tour; I just know it.'

Andy thinks about this for a moment and then he says, 'You're probably right. He needs a change. Maybe it's agoraphobia or something. Bit of fresh air will do him good.'

I'm glad I don't have to rely on Andy for anything much.

In the middle of all this the doorbell goes and there's a man on the step with eyes so bright they almost hurt. He leans in like an old-style musical hall turn.

'Need anything sharpened sir?' he says.

'No,' I say and start closing the door.

'Sure?' says he. 'Scissors, knives, machine blades? I'm very good. Reasonable rates.'

Marco comes out into the hall and sees the man too. Suddenly the man nips past me, going up close to Marco, and starts giving out a patter about the clever tools he has and what a pleasure it is to have a sharp implement. Marco's listening with a beatific expression.

'I'm sure we must have something for you to do,' Marco says, 'Don't we have anything Steve? Here is a man who really wants something to sharpen. Shouldn't that count for something Steve, in this place where we've forgotten how to want anything at all? You know the trouble with England, Steve? How would you like to come to New York with us?' he says to the man. 'There's probably a lot you could do over there.'

'Well,' says the man, 'I do have a sister in Buffalo.'

Suddenly Marco is all excited about going to New York, as long as the knife sharpener can come along. I don't say a word about visas or passports or plane tickets. I go into the bedroom and pack Marco's bag. Andy orders a taxi.

As we're getting into the taxi I manage to say to the knife sharpener through my teeth: 'The guy is not well. You come with us to the airport, see us to the departure gate, then I give you fifty quid and you disappear. Got it?'

'Who did you say you were?' says the man, not at all friendly. If he thinks he's going to Buffalo he's got another thing coming.

Andy sits in front with the driver. It's a terrible cab. I think Andy must have some sort of racket going with this company; I can't see why else he'd keep using them. Their cars are worn down to their frame, all torn upholstery and broken springs in the seats. The driver is explaining to Andy how he has just this minute wired the stereo directly to the car battery to stop it blowing a fuse. I can see the headlines already: mysterious motorway fire kills New Age pop poet, record company man, personal manager and knife sharpener. I am thinking of Jackie. I want to see her one more time, please don't let the stereo explode, Lord; I just want to see her and say thanks.

The knife sharpener is explaining to Marco how you get a nice finish on a pair of scissors. Andy and the taxi driver are talking cars: air bags and fuel injection and high performance engines. It's pathetic.

'You need to connect it to the aerial mate,' says Andy, cocking an ear at the terrible hiss coming out of the radio.

'No,' says the driver. 'It is connected but the aerial broke off yesterday, that's all. Seen the new Honda? They've got air bags on the passenger side now.'

'Good cars, Hondas,' says Andy. 'But fucking expensive on spare parts.'

'You've got to have a steady hand,' says the knife sharpener to Marco. 'One shake and you really mess up the line.'

I look out of the window. The roads are busy; full of people with places to go, things to do. We pick up speed for a bit so that the houses begin to run together in a red blur, then we slow again, waiting to turn off along the common and I see a woman with plastic gloves, picking leaves out of the gutter and putting them into a bag. I've seen her before, pulling weeds from the pavement, collecting stray cans and fag packets. She will nip into your front yard and put the lids back onto your bins after the bin-men have been. It's as if the world is a monstrous big house that she's struggling to keep on top of; busy, busy. It's work and then again it's not. Nobody asks her to do it. Nobody's paying her. What is it then? Pleasure? I think of Jackie again. How long have I known her? I forget now. When was the last time I looked at her properly? Really looked at her and said something that wasn't strictly necessary? Something nice? I must do that if we ever get to the airport alive. I try and remember her face.

We get to the airport and the taxi driver insists on taking our bags into the terminal for us. I want to get rid of him but he won't let go of the trolley. Marco is shrivelled up into his coat, looking a pale grey colour but I tell myself to stop worrying about that; once we get him over there we can work on piecing him together again. We can always cancel the first week till he's settled in, get him some pills or something. Andy shoots off to the left of me saying he's going to the toilet. The taxi man is streaking away in the wrong direction with the trolley, dreaming of a big tip. I can see Jackie ahead of us in the crowd. The taxi man is pushing the bags away from her, veering further to the right. And the knife sharpener says to Marco:

'Take this blade here for instance.' Out of the corner of my eye

I see him pull a knife from his inside coat pocket. He and Marco stop and look down at it; a stream of silver between them. 'This was my grandfather's knife and his grandfather's before that. And look at the blade on that.'

The taxi driver is getting further away in the crowd. I yell. He doesn't hear but Jackie does. I see her face turned towards me, small and tight as an apple. How many times have I seen her face, in how many different lights, and yet it seems new to me today. Suddenly I have the feeling that something is about to happen. She is going to tell me something. She has somewhere else to be. Something is going to happen. The taxi driver has stopped now, aware that he has lost us but not sure exactly where. Andy is at the top of the stairs, looking around vaguely. Marco and the knife sharpener stare at the blade.

Then Marco reaches out and takes the knife in his hand and I realise too late that I am looking in the wrong places. I am not doing my job. Marco pushes up his sleeve and strokes the blade along his arm. For a moment nothing, then a pure red line blooms on the skin. Somebody cries out; I'm not sure who.

Jackie is there. She has the knife away from him and she takes him in her arms. 'Marco,' she says. 'It's all right Marco. It's all right baby. You don't have to do this. You don't have to go this far. It's OK.'

They're all looking at me for some reason: Andy, the taxi driver, even the bloody knife sharpener. I can hardly believe it but they're looking as if it was all my fault. Their eyes are saying to me: Are you happy now? Is this what you wanted? As if I gave him the knife. As if I pressed it into his flesh.

*   *   *   *   *

So, I'm sitting in the unemployment benefit office a couple of weeks later watching the straggly lines of people move up to the windows to sign on. I have to wait to see one of the supervisors because they've lost my file. There is a little stall set up at the back of the room; a big man in a suit sitting at the table and a banner saying 'Enterprise Allowance Advisor'. You have to be on the dole for seven or eight weeks before you can do that scheme. I don't plan to be unemployed that long, so I look away again. Then I say to Jackie:

'Am I dreaming or is that a man on a unicycle by the door over there Jack?'

'It is a man on a unicycle, Steve,' says Jackie, laughing.

She's taken time off from work to come here with me which is good of her, though I can't quite get rid of the feeling that she's like someone going round unplugging things and switching off the lights before leaving a place. I'm not sure how I feel about that. It's the waiting that gets me I suppose. She tells me that she's been to visit Marco at his mother's place. Perhaps I should get in there first; say I want a fresh start, a clean break. I could get another flat, buy some new clothes, cut my hair.

We both look at the man on the unicycle. He's a pleasant looking bloke with wild hair and day-glo stripes on his trainers, as if that is ever going to stop him getting killed in the traffic. He pauses in the doorway for a minute, holding onto the frame, all relaxed and casual, scanning the room.

Then he sees the Enterprise Allowance stand and his eyes light up. He launches himself off the door frame and out into the room. He goes forward in quick little bursts, around the chairs, a quick detour behind the display boards to get momentum, then he stops and rocks back and forth for a minute, twisting and rocking on the spot to keep steady, then another quick dash around the ashtrays, and into the open country beyond, weaving very fast across the lino tiles.

'Welcome,' says the Enterprise Allowance man, looking like he's really pleased to see this bloke, but then that's his job – pretending to want to help these characters. He gets up and takes a step with a big, easy smile. He is waving a fistful of brochures, as if they are ever going to be useful to anybody. The man on the unicycle leans forward and falls off, very slow and controlled, in front of the desk.

'Welcome!' says the man in the suit. 'Welcome!'

'Nutters,' I say to Jackie. 'The world is full of them.'

But she is far away. She is somewhere else.

Adam j Maynard

HOLIDAY

I'll tell you what I really want to
do. What I really want to do is
to walk down St Tropez
boulevard in a bear costume,
smoking a huge Monte Christo
cigar from Cuba. I want to drive
a fifties Mercedes through the
streets of Rio wearing a lurid
Hawaiian shirt and a Panama. I
want to create havoc at apres-ski
parties at chalets in the Swiss
alps. I want to dive off the end
of jetties in beautiful Spanish
fishing towns into the sparkling
Mediterranean. I want to have
pedalo races off the coast of
Brittany. I want to get drunk on
cheap French wine and start
little revolutions on the
campsites. Power to the camper.
Campers come together and
revolt!

palace of nicotine

from the novel
their heads are anonymous

by alistair gentry

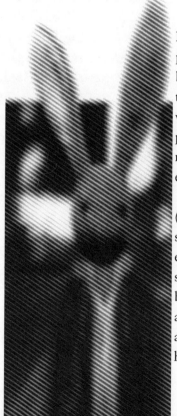

Doggo drifted aimlessly into a bar, picked up a girl and she took him back to her hotel room where they talked a bit and then made love without a word. But all this took place inside the Bigger Amusement World where nothing could ever be that simple.

The Olde Englishe Pub (luckily somebody had seen some sense and thought better of a third extraneous letter E) had a bar and so, technically speaking, was a bar. Its drinks were served in authentic tankards—unknown in any real pub at any point in history—by buxom within the boundaries of a family environment English serving wenches who were mostly French. It had a low beamed ceiling, but not so low as to lead to concussion followed swiftly by civil action, unless you were unusually tall. The top of Doggo's head brushed the beams when he stood. The antique books and rustic hurricane lamps were superglued to the shelves and the dartboard had never been used because there were no darts. The place was full of haggard fathers in hiding, drained by days or weeks of unrelenting and unwanted time with their normally decorative wives and children. What the Olde Englishe Pub did not have was alcoholic drinks. Or ashtrays. The kind of no ashtrays which means there are no ashtrays for a reason and the reason is because you are not under any circumstances going to smoke in here pal.

Doggo sat on a bar stool for an indeterminate length of time with his head tilted towards the ceiling, not even sure of what he was looking at or what he expected to see up there.

'It's far too clean, isn't it? That's the problem with this whole place.'

Doggo turned his head, taking her in with one swift imperceptible scan. Strong legs, long legs in 501s, almost too tightly belted like a kind of denim corset. White teeshirt. No attempt to hide the fact that her breasts were very much there and worth looking at, but not screaming out get a load of my knockers either. Tired hair fell without enthusiasm around a face that wasn't contemporary feminine. The kind of face normally described as striking; the kind of face that nobody would necessarily pick but would be quite pleased to have if that was the way things turned out.

'I'm sorry?' said Doggo.

'I noticed you'd been looking at the ceiling for a while, and I kind of wondered what you might be looking at,' she said, starting to put her hands in her pockets but then thinking better of it and placing them gently between the beer mats on the bar instead.

'Then I realised what it was. It's the wrong colour. It's too clean. It's like practically everything here. Everything's too clean. Pub ceilings should be... amber.'

Doggo nodded.

'You've been watching me.'

There was no accusation in his voice, just a statement of fact. Strange for him to be noticed at all, let alone to be watched with such obvious interest. She looked at him with a slight smile deciding whether or not to show itself fully on her lips.

Making dotted lines with his eyes, he indicated the Silk Cuts peeping out of her right hand jeans pocket.

'I'm dying for a fag.'

She leaned forward slightly, almost resting her chin on an elegant hand. And smiled.

'I knew you would be. Come back with me to my palace of nicotine and you might be in luck,' she said.

•

Ruthie sat on the edge of the bath in the en suite of her new fluorescent lit hotel room. Fluorescent strips are not designed to flatter anything except meat and electronic appliances, yet Doggo revised his estimate of her upwards. Ruthie, wearing only lipstick, was strikingly beautiful.

Deliberate in her actions, Ruthie slowly pulled the pack from her pocket and placed it down on the cistern lid beside her. She searched for her lighter in her other pocket and found it. She picked up the cigarettes, almost in slow motion, drew one out and lit the tip gently, taking a short drag with a slight nose exhale. She put the lighter down on top of the pack. Then, finally, she took the first full drag, holding it in and then exhaling a perfect cone of downward smoke.

'I bet there's some things you'd like to ask me,' she said.

Doggo had been transfixed. He shook his head slowly.

'I don't have a clue what I'm supposed to be asking you. It's just...'

They had gone together to Ruthie's hotel room, to the frank but inexplicable displeasure of the man at the front desk, the Bigger International's self-appointed arbiter of morality. They had told each other their names and ritually exchanged mutterings of I'm not in the habit of doing this. Doggo found a strange growth in

Ruthie's jeans.

'... It's just outside my area of expertise, that's all.'

Ruthie was a transsexual. Very clearly in the trans stage of being sexual.

'Show me,' Doggo said and Ruthie did, pulling her teeshirt up over her head and slipping out of her bra to show the still soft, pink scars of the augmentation mammoplasty. The feeling produced in him by the sight of her altered and scarred, very beautiful body was far beyond anything of its kind that Doggo had ever felt before. It was memory and recognition, only barely remembered and half imagined. Like something in a dream. The sort of dream that comes back to you at random, unexpected moments making you wish you could dream it again and return to the place in your mind where it has been living secretly all the time.

She didn't want to look him in the face, so she inspected the inoffensive royal blue Flotex carpet, as if the answers to unspoken questions could be found written there in scuff marks and vacuum cleaner stripes.

'I suppose it wasn't a very nice thing to do,' she murmured, 'not to tell you before. Before you found out for yourself. I feel bad about it.'

'But the world's full of people who do things that aren't very nice,' he said, taking her girl slender wrist in one broad hand.

Ruthie looked into Doggo's face as he leaned against the sink, then over his shoulder at herself in the mirror.

'Or have things done to them that aren't nice either. So what?'

Ruthie looked deeper into his hard face with a strange unreadable expression on her own.

'I'm just so used to being greeted like I was some kind of terrible monster. Some kind of scum. I suppose that's why I ended up here, of all the places I could have gone to,' she said, turning over Doggo's hand and comparing the tininess of her own in wonder. 'Just to be amongst the cartoons. Because I feel like one myself.'

'I bet you make some people who were born women sick that they don't look like you.'

'And some people think that what I've done—' looking down at herself, her creation, '—is sick.

Against nature.'

'Of course it's against nature,' Doggo said, studying Ruthie's face closely for seams or flaws and finding none. 'So is Maggie Gnu.'

'What do I do now?' she said. 'What do we do now?'

'Tell me,' whispered Doggo, and Ruthie did, perched on the edge of the bath.

'I'm having my body surgically altered to become more beautiful and more feminine,' she said. 'I know I'm capitulating to a particular set of norms imposed by the white Anglo-Saxon media, but it's just something that I feel like I have to do.

'It's because I think that the body finally can't be touched by all our cynicism and shifting systems of belief that we no longer have any faith in anyway,' she said. 'My own body is the only place where there's any basis for real values or real change.

'I remember lying awake at night with the memory of a boy's skin on the tips of my fingers,' she said. 'Something innocent, lying there thinking of some innocent forbidden place like the curve of his shoulder or the grooved skin where the elastic of his pants cut into his waist.

'I want to mould myself,' she said. 'Shape myself into something that was never here before. I want to be myself, I want to be myself now and for the rest of my natural life which ergo means forever.

'Some of the men I've slept with,' she said, 'have been effeminate beyond the most desperate dreams of any woman. Some of the men I've slept with didn't even know that the Village People were gay.'

Doggo noticed that there wasn't enough air in the room, something not powerful enough about the air conditioning. He kissed Ruthie's mouth, which tasted like coffee and cigarette breath, slightly sour. Gently drew his fingers along the semicircular cicatrices which ran beneath her new breasts.

'Let's turn the television off,' he said, leading her by the hand out of the bathroom.

Ruthie looked at the blank, inert screen and then at him.

He shrugged. 'I thought... I could hear voices. I thought the telly was on when we came in. I thought I could hear a news report, a news flash or something.'

'Could've been in the next room,' she said, pointing out the cord which lay limp and unplugged against the wall. 'I didn't hear anything.'

Doggo sat slightly hunched on the edge of the bed with his meat hands hanging between his knees.

'It doesn't matter,' he said. 'Come here. It doesn't matter. There's so much of it that you hear it even when it's not there. It's like you don't need an aerial any more to pick up TV transmissions. And I think telly is responsible for everything that's bland, boring and completely fucked in the world.'

She sat beside him, thigh to thigh.

'Are you a reader, then?'

'No. No. I don't read any books,' Doggo replied, looking genuinely surprised to hear the words coming out of his mouth. 'I don't think I ever even touch them or hold them, now that I think about it. It's like they're alien objects. Like I'm afraid of them. Afraid of receiving information because I might not like it, or I might not like what I feel I have to do because I know a certain thing. In my life, I mean, not in my job.

Because my job is information—'

Ruthie took hold of his hands again. Fascinated by his hands.

'One thing,' she said quietly. 'I'm not a woman trapped in a man's body. I'm a man with tits. Or a woman with a dick.'

Doggo looked thoughtful for a moment, his eyes almost lost in his face, heliograph signals in flesh valley.

'That's cool,' he said.

The cockroach sitting on Ruthie's suitcase interrupted the Sisyphean task of cleaning itself to watch them while they kissed hard and time stood still as they made love. Tactfully, the roach kept to itself any opinions it might have had about the pointless eroticism which took up so much of a mammalian life.

With extreme nonchalance the woman placed her champagne flute on the buffet table. Her camouflage plastic kimono contrasted sharply with her bald head and the glass rings piercing her septum. She bent her knees as if checking her fishnet stockings, and picked something up from the floor.

I can see her, but no one else does. My observation corner is the best spot in this large, animated room. I can see without being seen. The ideal, really. Especially at a party like this one.

Quickly she brings her fingers close to her lips. She throws a glance across the packed hall.

I can see she is nervous.

She opens her mouth and eats her salmon paté canapé.

‹‹The collision with planet Earth is expected to take place in a few hours. The satellite is travelling at the speed of 300 metres a second towards one of the most populated areas of London, roughly West 10 and West 11. Do not panic. Follow the instructions of your local Emergency Evacuation Plan advisor and nobody will be hurt. Every step is being taken to minimise impact on landing. High Density Defence Rockets have been programmed to intercept the satellite, disintegrating it and dispersing its fragments in the atmosphere. I repeat, there is no reason to panic, everything is under control.

‹‹Live mondovision coverage of the event will commence on this channel after the consumer advice break. Join us then.››

This morning, when Bee looked at herself in the bathroom mirror, she noticed a slightly dark spot on her back. Nothing alarming. Nothing more than a shadow, but still quite visible, it neatly defined a portion of her skin. A transversal stripe, a couple of inches wide, curved and asymmetric, reminding Bee vaguely of a serpent. She tried to scrape it off with a generous dose of soap. She retrieved a pumice stone that had lived untouched in a corner of the bath-tub for as long as she could remember, almost part of the décor, and scratched at her skin.

But even the stone could not get rid of that unusual, frankly disturbing, shadow.

It was late, Bee had to run to the art college where she worked, so she postponed the matter for later investigation.

Unzipping her rubberised overall (from a market stall that specialised in old AstroWear gear from space explorations of the nineties), Bee remembered the mark. Now, every single student in the life drawing class would see it. Some student might interrogate her about the strange shadow on her body. After all, as their life model her job was to be stared at and analysed in every detail. Her body could not avoid the two dozen nosy eyes waiting for her to strip, because, whatever it was on her back, it was unmistakably growing.

By this point half her back was covered by shadowy stripes, all approximately of the same size and the same snake-like shape.

I know what she picked up from the floor. And I know also that she ate it with pleasure. Like a gourmet, I would say. I know well the joyful enjoyment of tasting (especially when you least expect to) your favourite delicacy. The mouth waters, the eyes shine, if you were a dog you would be lolling your tongue over the floor. When the papillae are invaded by the unmistakable taste of crunchy bits melting with juicy filling it is like floating into a heavenly instant of complete fulfilment. That is what she experienced. The bald woman, I mean.

Few of you so far, I keep repeating to myself. Few of you so far. But more, many more to come, I am sure. It was predicted centuries ago, it was prophesied and written down in those ancient dusty papers that no one uses any more, kept in the City General

Library. It has been dreamt of, it has been feared.

And now, just now, it is happening.

‹‹As we speak, no human victims have been recorded. The satellite collided last night at 3.17am hitting the main building of a deserted tube station. The impact created a crater 20 metres in diameter, no more than 5 metres deep. A local entrepreneur has already sought permission to build a water-sports centre in this natural swimming pool. Again, we repeat, no victims reported. The emergency has ceased and life is back to normal. Thank you for being with us. That is all for now, good afternoon.››

The nurse looked at Bee with motherly eyes and then she spoke in a soft whisper. Yes, the doctor could see her this morning. If she just took a seat, it would be a matter of minutes. While Bee browsed the websites of the **Disabled Today Review**, her mind wandered in circles, puzzled by the mutation taking place in her body. Strangely enough, she was not worried at all. Rather the opposite, she would have said. Inside of her, somewhere, something thrilling was happening.

The doctor was swift, inexpressive and

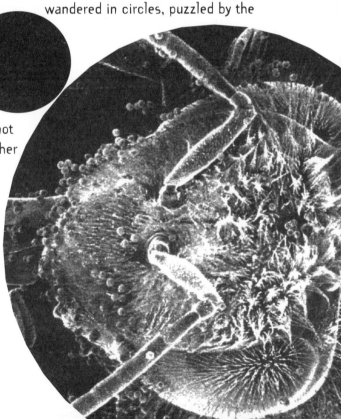

obviously bored. He diagnosed stress and gave Bee the number of a Healing Centre called **Wipe Your Vibe** (run by his sister-in-law).

Bee went home and disposed herself in observation of the next change. She decided that whatever was happening to her it was something to be proud of.

From my observation corner I can spot the movements of most of the guests. Now they are approaching the long table where dinner will be served in a moment. I still can see the bald woman. She is talking animatedly with a man dressed in white who is sipping from a bright green drink. Celery juice, I suppose, giggling to myself.

It is dinner time now. I crawl back into the corner where those succulent pastry crumbs I gathered before are waiting for me. Moving my anterior legs I make a tiny ball out of them, and finally, I start to eat.

Bee is ready to go out. She is wearing a specially made outfit tonight, as this is a very special evening. Her shiny black catsuit makes her body look stunning, and she is aware of it. Another glance over her shoulder at the mirror: perfect. Cutting the back off her catsuit worked brilliantly. The black stripes covering her back are impressively beautiful; the mark of the mutant. The image reflected in the mirror is that of a hybrid creature, someone or something in between human and animal. After all, this is going to be the future, isn't it?

Since the satellite collision, more and more people have begun to experience changes in their appearance. Nothing serious. Just details, some feelers here, a pair of wings there. Or, as in Bee's case, a mimetic coverage, similar to the pattern of a zebra.

Glancing for the last time at the mirror, Bee goes outside, stops a cab and half an hour later makes her gorgeous debut at the annual dinner party of the Entomological Food Society.

Mark Dove

Mmmmmmmmmmmmmmmmmmmmm
mmmmmmmmmmmmmmmmmmmmm
Nik shaves your head. The clippers
hum like a mystic and you watch the
downy little hairs drift onto the
newspaper. Hair is dead messy stuff
that gets in the way. You can't
understand it, how a giro could just
disappear like that. Nik finishes and
you change places. The clippers are
sturdy and satisfying in your hand
like a gun. Like you imagine a gun
would feel.

Catering assistant required in
popular fast food restaurant, must
be motivated and disciplined.

marc bolan stole your giro

simon lewis

Everyone wants
fitters or joiners.
What's a
joiner? Maybe
you're a joiner. No, you remember
Embryohead watching you standing
alone at the side of the playground
and saying you're not a joiner are
you? You have sexual fantasies about
film characters. Pissed up, you and
Nik break some windows.

You find a space lego man in the
gutter and take it home. It still has
the aqualung thing on the back, and
the spaceship logo on its chest.
Look, says Nik, a police raid. The

back window of your flat faces directly onto the front of another, identical, block of flats. It's like a view of graph paper. Up in the far left corner, around C7, you see a flurry of little figures. You twist the helmet off the space lego man. A man in green boxer shorts is being dragged away with his arms handcuffed behind his back. The top of the space lego man's head is flat, with a raised round bump where the helmet clicks on.

You can tell it's morning by the light filtering under the curtain. Pearl the Cow talks to Daisy the duck, trying to convince her not to fly south for the winter. You don't have any money. Brian Cant comes on with a straw in his mouth. All the colours are bleaching out, everything is going grey. Nik says Pineapple chunks.

You want to squeeze your blackheads in the mirror above the vegetables at the supermarket. You wish you weren't too gutless to be a shoplifter. Nik is a great shoplifter. But he doesn't look like a shoplifter. You have a dishonest head. You don't believe in vitamins. You draw on the faces in the TV guide.

Nik's other offences are taken into consideration. You go and see him in prison. You sit at a table with a wobbly leg. Nik says he lies around bored and stoned all day. It's like the flat. He runs his hand over the new bristles on your head. Like stroking a dog.

You never find your giro. Do me with your hairy cock moans Princess Leia. Chewbacca howls and shows his teeth.

"where's my audience darling?"
spotlight on decadence
and dreams
moving with limousine style and glittering
ambition

wanting to live way beyond my means
express style of course
superficial with champagne

and when the words come you can't deny them

i'll be ready — dressed for fame, a street diva
a backstreet goddess looking for that cruising star
pose and portray that alter ego baby

i gloss my lips and **kiss** the air

move over because
it's party time and i'm out with the glamour boys

deviant in my delight gatecrashing with a smile
give me all the attention you possess and i'll still take more
i've got something i think you'll like
i'm feeling so very frenetic, step into my limelight if you dare and

let's explode together

throw caution under my stilettos and i'll walk all over it
and "la-de-da" i'll say to you
let's not take ourselves too seriously
and "where's my audience" i'll say to you
what i'd give for your applause
am i too old yet?

anna landucci

1

If I can just get my wife to have sex with next-door's dog, everything will be alright.

Americancola[2]
Richard Guest

"Jasmine."

"Yes."

"About what we talked about last night..."

"Not now, Dan. Ben Lester's on in a minute."

"But, Jasmine..."

"Dan!"

She loves Ben Lester. He's a woman-of-a-certain-age pornstar, I suppose. He must be; Little Eddy isn't that interested. No, all we hear from her is:

"Ooh. Look Dan. Hasn't he lost weight?"

POLAROID® 3 W
10543058054

I turned the volume up.

Interviewer: Suck Day 2, Ben. They're saying it's your best yet...

Ben Lester: Well, Bob. When I've got a sore cock and a sore throat, I know I've given the best performance I can.

Interviewer: And that happened this time?

Ben Lester: Yes.

Jasmine turned round. She was glowing. "Thanks, Dan." She

likes it when I do these little things for her. "What was it you wanted to talk about, love?"

"Well, Jerry's dog."

"Not again. That mangy Alsatian."

"It's not mangy. It's quite clean. It's a nice dog. Jerry's got it well trained…"

"I've told you before, Dan. We're not having a dog."

"I don't want a dog."

"Well, why do you keep on about it, then?"

"I just want you to see it."

"No. I don't like dogs."

"So, have you squared it with the wife, then?"

"No. Not really."

"Dan. For fuck's sake. I've nearly clinched the deal. If you want to pull out of it, we have to do it now. You know what their contracts are like. Are we going to have to pull out? If we are, tell me now. Otherwise we'll have USA1 lawyers climbing all over us for the rest of our lives."

"She'll come round. When she knows what it's for."

"She'd better. Little Ed still wants the David Acidy Link subscription, yeah? Well, if we pull this off, she'll have it."

‹‹Can you guess where we are, kids? That's right. We're at the funfair. It's closed at the moment, because it's very early in the morning. Doesn't the Flume Ride look like fun? Perhaps I'll have a go on that later. Over there, though. See those trees. That's natural cover, if ever I saw it. Just behind there is some good soft earth. That's where I'm going to bury the body…››

"What's this you're watching, my sweet?"

"Dan. Don't call me that. You're not Johnny Moron, you know. Anyway, that show's really old."

"You don't like Johnny Moron, anymore?"

"No. 'S dogshit. Johnny Moron is way out. Cherry said. This is the new show."

"What is it, Eddy?"

"Live Killer. 'He's a real artist.'"

"Oh."

"Don't say I'm not grown up enough. I'm ten years old. I'm a woman, now."

"OK. But you do still like David Acidy, don't you? I mean, your mum and me..."

"David Acidy is God."

"Good."

"You are going to get me David for my birthday. You better. I can't keep going over to Cherry's to watch it, you know. 'Sembarrassing."

"You know your mum and me don't have much credit, Eddy."

"It's only $2000.99. Cherry said. And if you don't get it..."

We built the set in Jerry's apartment. Well, he built it. I'm not much good with flat-packs. Jerry ordered the Wendy House set, which is like a miniature room; lots of flowers on the walls, and a little old-fashioned window. It's very clever. Jerry thought it would bring in an element of comedy, what with Jasmine being the size she is and everything.

"It's just another angle, Dan. Another selling point. Dexter from next door is going to bring his lights the day after tomorrow. So, I think it's time Jasmine met Adolf. What are you looking so worried about, Dan? This time next week, we'll be rolling in dollars."

"Did you see that yesterday?"

"Uh huh."

"When he walked round the back of our couch, we were convinced his hair-piece was going to come off. He just needs to get some better glue."

"Dan."

"Yes."

"Adolf wants to meet Jasmine."

"Get that animal out of here."

"But, Jasmine..."

"The food man is coming."

"What's that got to do with anything?"

"I am not being seen by the food man with a dog. It's unclean."

"Oh, Jasmine. Don't be ridiculous. The food man won't care about that. All he does is deliver."

"Don't call me ridiculous, and get that fucking animal out of here. Or I want a divorce, okay?"

"What, again?"

"What did you say?"

"Nothing."

The food man called. We ate Meditteraneo. Little Eddy and her new boyfriend, Crazy Craig, ate American. That stuff gives me indigestion. And Americancola is too fizzy. I don't know how they drink it. I shut Adolf in the bathroom while we ate. He made a lot of noise. But Civil War USA2 was on, so I don't think Jasmine heard.

Jerry came over in the last quarter. We went into the bathroom.

"Why are we in here, Dan?"

"I don't want Jasmine to hear."

"What? You haven't introduced her yet? Dan, I don't believe this. What the fuck are you playing at? I've had Guy from USA1 on. The deal is go. We have to do this now, or we can both forget food for the next ten years."

"Stop shouting. Even if Jasmine hears, I definitely don't want Little Eddy to."

"Where is she?"

"She's in her bedroom with Crazy Craig. I think

they are probably trying to fuck."

"Trying is the word. Do you remember what it was like when you were ten? It's not like the ads..."

"Jerry. Look, I think we're going to have to convince Jasmine together. Have you got last night's Watch Wives?"

"Yes."

"Can you bring it over in half an hour? I'll try and introduce her to Adolf."

"I just don't believe this, Dan."

"Well, we're in it now. We just have to do the best we can."

Jerry went home.

Crazy Craig came streaking out of Ed's room, with his arms full of clothes. He turned to me with tears in his eyes and said, "I can't get no satisfaction." Little Eddy came stumbling after him. But he was gone by the time she reached the door.

"Wasn't that a Pink Gates song?"

"Uh-huh. Craig's crazy. Pink Gates is way out. Look. I got his VR goggles, though."

"Can you pick anything good up on them?"

"Dunno. They're Mark 2. Old. Craig's mum and dad have less credit than you, even."

<hr>

2

Hollingsworth's coming. I know what it's about — the end of my last link. I was really roaring. I think it was a minor, but you never know with Hollingsworth. Pammy's done what she can; she got most of the dust out of the apartment, but there's probably enough residue on the furnishings to get me busted. Oh, why, oh why did I get into this business. I could have stayed in the retail department; even after Semper told them about my face and my butt. I could have opted out. But I wanted to be a star. Fuck, I need some dust.

"Senor Acidy, you have visitors."

"Send them up, Pammy. Then you can go."

I watch Pammy talking to Hollingsworth on the monitor. He's got three men with him. This is obviously more serious than I thought. I don't even remember what I said last night. Three seems a little excessive.

The buzzer.

Quick check. No evidence. Nothing on the suit; pupils are probably dilated. Too late to...

3

"I can't leave the street, Jerry."

"It's your fault the dog got out. Come on, or we're going to lose him. He's nearly at the junction. Come on."

"But I haven't left the street since Little Eddy was born."

"Come on. I think I know where he's going. He's done this once before."

"You've seen Today, Jerry. It's not safe outside."

"What are you talking about? Look around you. Do you see anybody?"

Jerry walked off. What could I do? I had to follow him. After all it was partly my fault that Adolf had got out. Mainly it was Jasmine's fault. She was the one that had screamed. Did he run. You don't expect a dog to do that, I thought they were more, well, vicious. No. It just made this funny high-pitched noise and ran. Jerry must have seen it from his window. Adolf running faster than Crazy Craig. Jasmine was still screaming when I got out on the street. It's funny. I thought she would have been pleased that we were finally going to be able to shut Little Eddy up about David Acidy. But no. She wouldn't even do this little thing. So it's going to be all hell from Little Eddy, and no food for a month.

"I want half of any food you've got left."

"Look, let's find Adolf before we start on that."

"Maybe I could trade him, or I wonder if they'd let me swap my Link for food, if I promise never to call them again."

"Shut up, Jerry."

"Well, you've ruined everything. You and your fucking wife. I was going to be a star."

"What, based on an excerpt in Watch Wives? Get real hombre."

"But USA1 never gives anyone a second chance. You've seen the ads. That's it for me."

Well, look at you in your USA1 suit.

"Hello, Mr Hollingsworth."

The three goons fan out, covering the three doors out of the living-room.

"Sit down, David."

"I'd rather stand."

"Sit down."

I sit on the Cerullo.

"You know what? You're an idiot."

"If this is about last night..."

"Don't interrupt me, David." Hollingsworth turns to address the goons, "Mr Acidy's not going anywhere, boys. Relax, get yourselves a drink." And then to me, "You're not going anywhere, are you? Good, because we need to talk, David."

He sits down opposite me. The leather creaks. Between the cushion and the arm, I anticipate a bag of dust. There isn't one.

"What's the matter?"

"Nothing."

"Nothing. I see." He strokes a crease out of his trouser suit and, without taking his eyes off me, says, "Lenny, fix me a JD, no ice." Then he reaches into his jacket pocket and pulls out a pair of Mark 5s.

"Put them on."

I put the goggles on.

<< *The end of my link. I look wired. My hair is losing its cone. Their stormtrooper costume looks awkward on me. Close-up: face, sweating in the polychromatic blaze. My mouth opens a fraction, but nothing comes out. Close-up: eyes, glistening; pupils, dilated. Close-up: crotch, hard. None of this is a problem. And now I'm mouthing my words as they come back to me, "This is all so fucking ugly." For a moment the camera stays close on my face. Then there's a quick dissolve; and the Johnny Moron Saturday Show Ad comes on* >>

"Not a pretty sight, eh, David."

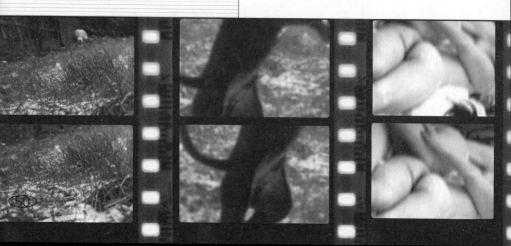

5

I really started to get nervy when we reached the crossroads. My hands went all wet.

"I'm anxious, Jerry."

"You watch too many Med-slots."

"But the sun's hurting my eyes."

Across the widest stretch of concrete I have ever seen, Adolf stood next to a marker-post, with his back leg cocked at a funny angle, and his tongue going in and out of his mouth.

"Adolf!"

The dog looked over at us, finished making water, and sat down. Jerry twisted his mouth into a smile, and said, "I hope he doesn't think this is a game."

"Thanks, Lenny. Right, so you have to agree that that was a pretty stupid thing you did last night, David. We know you've got a drugs problem. We can tolerate that. If it gives you a hard-on, well, it's good for you and it's good for business. As long as the pre-teens are wetting their pants, we're happy, but what you said last night was just plain stupid."

"Mr Hollingsworth..."

"I told you, don't interrupt. Lenny, break one of his fingers."

Lenny comes over. He's at least a head taller than me, and twice as wide. When he puts his hand on mine, his touch feels reassuring (like that of a doctor); then he breaks the little finger on my right hand. I can't help screaming.

"You see, attitude: where does it get you? Nowhere. Unfortunately for us, you having an attitude presents us with a problem. If it was just the drugs it would be easy. You go to rehab for a few months, we show re-runs, you recover, you come back good as new. But you're dissatisfied. I don't know why and to be frank, I don't care. But once you're dissatisfied, you stay that way. I watched it happen with Pink Gates. You remember him? There was nothing we could do. Underneath we knew he wasn't happy, that sooner or later he would let us down. And of course he did. We know there's nothing we could do to make you feel better. And, David, once you've bitten the hand that feeds you, all you can do is keep on biting. And you've bitten us.

"Do you have any idea how many people were subscribing to last night's David Acidy show? You made us look bad right across two continents. Quite an achievement for a tiny little prick like you. I always said it was a mistake, having live performers, but the board don't agree. They think the kids would notice the difference. What do you think, David? It's ok, you can answer this time."

"I think they...would notice."

"Hmm."

I see Lenny twitch, by the bar. He can't wait to be let off the leash again. But Hollingsworth doesn't call him over, or move. He just sits there in contemplation.

They're going to kill me.

7

"I'm not going over there, Jerry. I've seen..."

"You have to, Dan, because you're going to hold him still, while I put his cable on. I don't know what you're worried about. I've been out here, oh, a hundred times, and nothing's ever happened. Relax, ok? And try not to fuck anything up, this time."

"Ok."

We crossed the road, which stretched out in three directions. Left: nothing. Ahead: Adolf. Right: nothing.

"Mr Hollingsworth, I have to tell you. I've had an implant put in. If anything should happen to me, I will still be broadcasting. If you hurt me any more than you have done already, it goes live at nine."

"Even if that was true, David, it doesn't really matter. Your slot's been reallocated. As far as USA1 is concerned the David Acidy Show is history. You're history. We don't take chances anymore. Not after Pink Gates."

He takes another sip of bourbon.

"What is it about you people? I mean, It's not as if you have any talent, so you can't possibly want artistic control. We made you. Your stupid hair-style, those clothes you wear, your lines, your voice; that's us, not you. And you get all the credit. From the subscribers, anyway. You get all the credit, and all that goes with it. Look around you. Aren't we generous enough? What do you want?"

He brushes off his trousers and stands up. "It's beyond me. Lenny, kill the son-of-a-bitch."

Lenny starts forward, but I've got my blade out of my jacket, so he slows a little, looking to Hollingsworth for guidance. "What are you waiting for?" Lenny reluctantly lopes towards me.

"Come on then, you stupid fuck. Come and kill me." I wave the blade at him, keeping my eye firmly on the other two. Neither of them has made a move yet. I start backing towards the window. It's a three-storey drop, but the garbage-sacks should break my fall.

Why, oh why didn't I buy a gun when I had the opportunity?

Hollingsworth: "Ok boys, break the place up. Any dust you find, you can keep. Hurry up, Lenny. We got a dozen appointments today."

Lenny makes a grab for the knife. I slash his hand. He doesn't like it, but he doesn't make a sound. He picks up the Art Deco lamp off the coffee-table, breaks off the shade, and continues his advance. Then I see Hollingsworth reaching inside his jacket. Everything slows down. I can hear everything...Lenny's heavy footfalls on the carpet...the hairs on Hollingsworth's neck brushing his shirt collar as he turns to face me...the click of a safety-catch going off...myself screaming...the hammer going down.

BOOM.

The bullet grazes my ear and breaks the spell. I throw myself backwards. The window breaks easily.

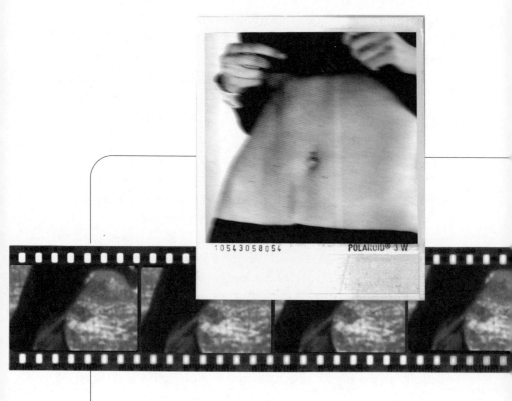

9

I got my hand round the dog's neck, but my palms were still slippery.

"Hurry up with the cable, Jerry."

"I'm trying."

Then I saw it. Down the road to the right, behind a broken cyclone fence...Green. Bright green grass. You hardly ever see that. There's some on the ground sometimes, in Civil War USA2, but it's more of a brown colour.

I saw the green, and I heard this noise, like something fast, like a big transporter, getting closer. I don't know what happened next, whether I let go or he pulled too hard, but Adolf got loose. The food man's van streaked past with a terrific bang.

A weird, strangulated sound came out of Jerry. I remember the back of the food man's cart getting smaller to my left. Then Adolf was lying on his side, on the concrete. Something like a snake or maybe a new tail, had grown from his stomach. We went over and looked at him. Not much was left of his head, but the way his teeth showed through the broken face made it look like he had a big, cheeky smile.

Jerry fainted.

I went home.

10

There's a light on upstairs. The Man, Henry is home.

He lets me in. I tell him what's happened. He says he's sorry to be losing one of his best customers, and agrees to give me one last blast, gratis. Fuck, am I grateful. But then I paid for this apartment (David's personal expenses), so I suppose he owes me one. While he sets up, I try to make small talk.

I'm so excited my hands are shaking, holding the toke tube. The water rushes in. I watch the bubble rising up the pipe, in slowmo, gathering air as it climbs towards my waiting mouth.

Closer. Closer...

MMMMMMMMMMMMmmmmmmmmmmmmmmmmmmmmmmmm

wildwildwildwildwildwildwildwildwildwildwildwildwildwildwild

IT ALL HAPPENS AT ONCE

KERRY LEE POWELL

The hoover breaks, the washing machine dies, a drop of undiluted bleach flies into my eye as I scrub the toilet. It all happens at once, as my grandmother used to say, remembering the dust bowl years on the prairies when her father rode the trains up and down the

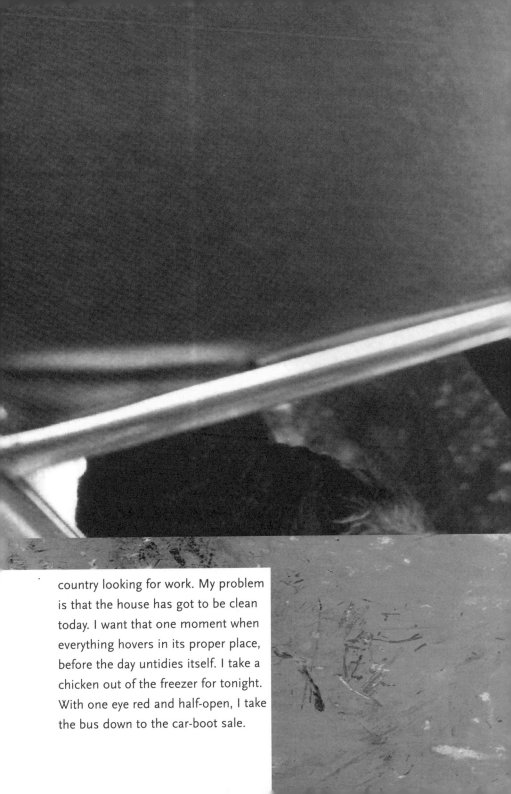

country looking for work. My problem is that the house has got to be clean today. I want that one moment when everything hovers in its proper place, before the day untidies itself. I take a chicken out of the freezer for tonight. With one eye red and half-open, I take the bus down to the car-boot sale.

As the bus pulls away from me, I realise that I have abandoned my half-read book on board. I picture the book's winding city tour as I stand empty-handed, frozen in mid-passage almost at the novel's exact centre, that last paragraph blurring and indecipherable because of my painful eye.

I often wonder about the cosmic ordering of the universe. Last week, the market was full of hoovers; this week, as if responding to a subliminal command, the theme is shoes. Wide old men's shoes and high heels. I touch them and remember the first time, working as a waitress, I noticed these inane shaping patterns; days when every other diner asked for, oh, just a chicken salad. The grimaces in the kitchen, the chef screaming: why today? Herds, I used to whisper to myself back then. Herds. Now, as I walk through the market another pattern emerges: toys. Not the faceless rubber dolls that typically inhabit this market but electronic toys, the latest in technology when I was a kid. I stand transfixed. Gleaming black toys with red, white, blue, yellow buttons that lit up a blurry Christmas twenty years ago when that same toy sat revered, batteries not included. A birthday space saucer, and on another stall, a silver plastic Star Wars tower. Time machines!

I am transported, but the few children I see do not even glance at them. This is my past, I want to say, spread across this market-place – as if a friend was yawning at me while I talked them through a photograph album.

No hoovers. I can't stop myself from buying a tiny wooden rocking horse with a cheerful,

stupid expression. I never had a rocking horse, I say to myself and tuck it in my bag. Finally I see the hoover curled up like an afterthought in someone's car boot.

On the bus there is a child with a kitten scooped into her blouse. The pensioners smile and smile. I arrive home with my hoover in front of me, like it's a stately matron. Whenever I hoover I have strange thoughts. Today, as my cats fly off at the sound of its suction, I wonder for example why there are such things as cat years and dog years, whether it's because they perceive time on a different scale. Don't we all just live at once? I think of the whole world, and all its worries, all happening right at this moment. Finally, the house is clean. I will prepare dinner.

My boyfriend comes home. He says nothing about his job interview, and I know this means he won't succeed. He doesn't look into my eyes, doesn't see the one red one. He starts telling me about his dreams the night before. I listen to him and wait. As he is carried off more and more into his dream world while at the same time the sun sinks behind the conifers in next door's garden, I realise there will never be a perfect, synchronised moment to tell him that I am going to have an abortion. Very carefully my voice arrests his in mid-reverie. And then, the sound of the back door slamming and his feet pacing up and down on the concrete slabs outside.

Inside, my heart pumping, the refrigerator buzzing, and the chicken on the kitchen countertop, still defrosting.

about the authors

Matthew Astrop was born in N2, grew up in N11 and N6 and now lives in N8. He enjoys shopping in Brecknock Road, N7 and his favourite television programme is Animal Hospital.

Steve Aylett once made someone's head explode like in that film Scanners. His books *The Crime Studio* and *Bigot Hall* (Serif) are widely regarded as cries for help. A new entreaty, *Slaughtermatic*, is to be published by Four Walls Eight Windows.

Joanna Gallagher lives in London.

Alistair Gentry claims that a lifesize Kermit the Frog was once his role model. *Their Heads are Anonymous* (Pulp Books, 1997) is his first novel.

Ian Grant is working on another novel – not that the first one has been published yet.

Vicky Grut's short stories have appeared in various magazines and in the collection *How Maxine Learned to Love Her Legs* (Aurora Metro, 1995).

Richard Guest works in a London museum.

Tim Hutchinson lives in London and works as an illustrator.

Anna Landucci is an artist, singer, natural born hustler and glamour bitch — stay tuned for more of her work, which goes out under the name Blue.

Reuben Lane — are you out there?

Simon Lewis is permanently in transit.

Kevin Lloyd is a mod who works/used to work for a Government agency.

Betti Marenko is a hybrid creature who enjoys scanning skinscapes with its antennae. Founder of the in.sect.corp, Marenko is writing a non-fiction book *The Theory of Mutant Bodies*.

Adam j Maynard is saving up for a package tour of Europe's tackiest resorts.

Jeff Noon is living in Manchester. Is dreaming about escape. Is calling the first dream *Vurt*, the second *Pollen*, the third, *Automated Alice*. Is having a recurring Blurbs dream that will be called *Nymphomation*.

Kerry-Lee Powell had a brief but lucrative career as a teenage runaway and coincidentally later made a short film about teenage shoplifting.

Ainsley Roberts is a trainee poetic terrorist in thrall to the shadowy forces of Multimediocrity.

Nick Rogers was born in Berkeley, Gloucestershire in 1861. He has been unwell for some time.

raining shoes

tim hutchinson

Outside the train station a man was shouting 'God' over and over and everyone was spilling around him like he wasn't there. I stopped the car with a blast of music and got out. Then a hand in my stomach; a leather bag with gold straps, did I look like I needed one of those? A man going around and around me trying to sell me his travelcard. Only one pound, seemed like a good deal; but I was driving. Then, then, then, a moment of quiet before sirens. Wa wa wa wa wa wa... Shit, did you see that bottle smash?

Vegetables. Vegetables and I felt something mouldy underfoot. I think it was a fish. The light from the Iceland frozen food store made the people waiting at the bus-stop look ill.

I walked on through the greasy evening towards the cinema, through some people all coming the other way. Hadn't been there for years, it had just opened again. I remember going with my brother just after he had moved in. It was raining so we decided to go and sit through a triple bill. Don't know what we ended up seeing but it was better than staying in a cold flat watching rain up against the windows.

A girl slipped past smelling of chewing gum and I wondered where she was going. She pulled a brush through her hair as she walked. She was the kind of girl I would have fancied when I was fifteen. Hell I fancied her now, or I wouldn't have noticed her. She looked like she had spent a long time in front of the mirror, wearing new clothes and shoes that were straight out of the plastic bag, smelling new all over.

I felt like following her but I couldn't do it.

As she turned the corner out of view she looked content.

It was a good film. I enjoyed being there on my own. When the words started going up the screen in

darkness I sat and waited for everyone to leave so that I could be alone just a moment longer before launching myself into the street.

First I needed to piss and when I pushed the toilet door it released a strong smell of newness. I have a good sense of smell, people think it odd but I can even smell when a new piece of electrical equipment has been brought into a house. It is a sweet smell. Now I could smell the electric lights and the new chrome taps.

'Fucking hell man, these are the best toilets I have ever been in. Space 1999.'

The man standing at the urinal understood this. Being in such a cool shaped clean white place where the walls sloped into the ceiling was a thrill and it's not often you get to feel that way in a toilet. Everything was really bright with mirrors that made you look good so that when you came out you felt like you could say anything to anyone. And I did.

As I left the cinema a girl was leaning up against my car smoking. When I went over she looked at me hard. Kind of what the fuck do you want. Then she realised it was my car and went all sorry and said,

'I didn't mean to smoke around

your car.'

'That's all right,' I said, 'I don't mind smoke.'

Then she said, 'But it's drugs,' with a stupid accent.

Then I said, 'Get in the car then,' and fuck me if she didn't.

I started to drive and we ended up at a private view. A small white stairwell with nothing on the walls. Then a blonde woman opened the door to a room filled with people all standing around drinking gin and tonics. The room was filled with people I recognised but didn't know. People I have seen around, but this was going back a long way and I didn't care to go into all that. There were some people that I talked to and it seemed that they knew the girl too, which was weird, because she never said anything.

In the street again it felt like very soon it would begin to rain. Everyone had their winter clothes on. It was the first real week of proper cold weather. We were all feeling good in items of clothing that we had forgotten we had.

Following a couple of men into the pub, we talked with them for a while before a bell sounded at the back of the room and I remembered that I had burgled their house when they were out of the country.

We climbed into the car and driving was beginning to feel much better than being somewhere. I can't remember how many places we went. It was one of those busy evenings that must have given the impression my whole life was always like that and maybe she sort of liked it that way.

She said that she had felt the same thing about the toilets and then it turned out that she had been to see the same film as me. She was the girl that was on with some guy the whole way through, sitting right in front of me making me lose track of the film. When I asked where the guy was she said that she didn't care and that maybe this was a rebound, but fuck it she was having a great time.

'Why worry about things?' she laughed.

We dropped in on a party. I didn't know whose house it was, but the door had been open and then I saw Toby and he was in a good mood, good enough to give us a tab each. So off we popped into the night which was about to open out. I hadn't felt this good in ages. We could do everything. Finally it started to rain so I drove somewhere where we could eat. A little cafe with pictures of famous people on the walls; the kind of famous from being on the telly when you were a kid, people who meant fuck all now. We ate English school dinner food and she talked and talked. The woman who ran the place sat up at the back and listened in on everyone's conversations and her son practised card tricks on people as they stood to pay their bills. You could tell that he really really wanted it to be magic and him to be magic and he kept saying, it's magic, just to make sure.

We walked out into the street and it was pissing down now, really pissing down. Non-stop water right through us teeming from the tops of buildings in long heavy ropes. The water was moving the road down to the lights at the junction and there was no sound except the white noise hiss of wetness. Running to the car we found ourselves in a little backstreet that was being dug up. We stopped to peer into a huge hole. Rat city. Hundreds of them scrambling over each other to get away from the water that was slowly rising. All gnawing like hands coming out of the mud; but it was too slippery. They were drowning and floating like they had just been woken up by the rain to die.

Then I saw faces and memories and bodies and everything just kept fucking coming.

Then suddenly there didn't seem like there was much left to do. Neither of us felt like dancing or going into that scene. We must have been coming down because we were starting to want to come up again.

'Actually,' she said, 'I've got something at home.'

'What?'

'Can't remember, but I know it's something.'

'Shall we go then?' I said.

'Go.'

But I didn't know where and we didn't realise that we were going in the wrong direction until we were way off. So we stopped and had some chips. Then we wandered around the seven eleven trying to wake the security guard up by picking chocolate off the shelves and eating it; but nothing happened. I couldn't imagine me getting away with something like that. She screamed in the street and we were in Whitechapel. A moment ago we were halfway across London.

'Do you think it's breakfast time yet?'

'Looks like it.'

It was still raining but not nearly as hard. There was a faint light coming from somewhere. We thought it was dawn but it was the sign above the photographic shop. She looked cold but it was then that it kicked in again and she started running. I ran after her by a big pile of books that someone had left in the street, along with some old oil paintings of ships and fruit, all gold and red, the kind of shit that went with the wallpaper. Then in the middle of the pavement, spilling out of a soggy cardboard box, we saw hundreds of stilettos all mixed up with prices on their soles. I leaned in and picked out a red velvet one with a heel on it like a pencil. I wanted to find the other one to see what they looked like together. So we sorted through them and as we put our hands and fingers into them, they

paired off. She leaned over and picked a cream strapped pair with gold leather flashes across the toes. Then she ran over to one of the shops and put them on the doorstep. They looked like they'd been left out to be cleaned, like in old hotels.

We must have spent hours with the shoes. When we had finished, every doorway in the entire street had a pair of high heeled shoes on its step. It was a beautiful fairy tale and we almost wished that we could stick around to see the face of the first person to open their door to a crisp new pair of shoes.

I couldn't find the car. First I thought it had been nicked and started to freak, but just as I was about to punch a hole in a window she said, isn't that it there? I'd been kicking my own car window. Then I couldn't find the fucking keys. I was aching all over when an albino kid stopped in front of us on a pair of rollerblades and I wondered what he was doing out at this time of night.

It was only when we got in the

car, turned the blower on and steam started rising out of us, misting up the windows while we tried to think of what to do next, that we noticed just how wet we were.

Red lights all the way. Sometimes I get it right and ride them but that night I was out by a few seconds.

'Shit, this is it, we're here. Stop the car,' she screamed.

Then it was her turn to lose the key. I was starting to feel thirsty and I was shivering, needing coffee. I followed her through a hallway that just disappeared into a corner where the toilet was and I took a moment to splash some cold water on my face, wondering why the room had a line running through it from top to bottom, like it had been split in two and stuck together again.

She was standing in a long big kitchen, full of plants. I looked at the ceiling and the cornice seemed to stop suddenly

and then we were sitting in the front room gulping back coffee looking out onto glass roofs below. She took me upstairs; pointed to a small opening in the ceiling. Climbing up the ladder I watched her snake into a small dim room, half of it stolen by a slice of ceiling. As she collapsed onto the bed on the floor she flicked the TV on in one continuous motion. Not because she wanted to watch it but because, she said, the lightbulb had gone. I stood there, the flickering screen translating her face as she began taking her clothes off. She had a sports bra on, rain coming out the ends of her hair and falling onto a body I had never seen before.

'Aren't you wet too?' she said. Prompting me to join her.

I looked at the TV again. Rain is good, I thought, like in films when it can get you naked.

I am one of The Swimming Pool Girls. So long have I have inhabited this chlorinated, cobalt water that my jowls have started to develop gills. Erosive, scaly skin knits itself into my bathing costume. The flesh between my digits is fusing and I will soon own two fins for hands. My crinkled finger-tips and furrowed toes are forever saturated. My matted hair has grown up and over my swimming cap.

I am but one of many curious amphibians. Some of the older girls now have no nostrils, while the youngest ones come complete with permanently inflated water-wings.

As a group we are not enemies of The Changing Room Boys, just not yet friends, and although we are segregated by mosaic walls, all of us seem lodged at an age where those of the same sex are more alluring. Our own genitalia — on the cusp of germinating — captivate and fascinate us but it is our premature and extensive vocabulary which has probably separated the sexes forever.

All I know about the bewildering world of The Changing Room Boys is what I see through the misted up porthole in the door which connects to our pool.

S W I M M I N G
C H A N G I N G

Joanna Gallagher

8'

7'

6'

5'

4'

3'

2'

P O O L   G I R L S

R O O M   B O Y S

From where I stand — on tiptoes — I cannot see where their changing room ends. The floors and walls are lined with milky ceramic tiles, their edges turning sour. Rings of ochre discolour the sinks. Water seeps from corroding indigo pipes and emerald filaments sprout from the cracks. I often wonder what the aroma is like in there, something sultry I expect, but my sense of smell has been impaired by the noxious disinfectant of our foot baths, so I can't remember if sultry actually has a fragrance.

Growing out of the walls are rows of empty-stomach-like urinals. Although they are set too high to be put to their proper use, a scrawny boy can often be seen sitting cupped inside one. Portly, porcelain sinks stand in groups of four, vast enough to bathe in, or, as is often the case, for two to sandwich themselves in swapping secrets. The leaky brass taps which tower over them are used as foot-rests and the mould which flourishes around the dislodged bases gets stuck between their toes.

Then there are the two long rectangular baths sunk into the floor. One of these troughs is often surrounded by upright youths, uniform white pants drawn slightly under their pink buttocks as they simultaneously pee. This pastime causes much amusement as they play games with their spurts of piss; aiming at plug hole targets, measuring jets, collectively crossing their streams to create a champagne coloured fountain. The other bath is where they lie and chat, a tangled mass of damp legs and arms. Clad always in pallid briefs, the boys are impaired by the heat as we are by the cold; moisture drips from their downy bodies as they move about the shadows, and the steam in the air leaves them short of breath. Their skin, light-starved and translucent, resembles tissue paper suffused with purple-blue arteries, veins and capillaries.

We girls have lips and nails of mottled blue. Our bodies are scattered with goose-bumps which we try and shake off by diving in and out of the water. The conditions naturally affect our temperaments; because no one ever passes through the door I can only imagine the difference. Changing Room Boys are mostly quiet; lounging in tubs, coiled around pipes, languorously sprawled on the tiles. Sometimes they are all so still it's as

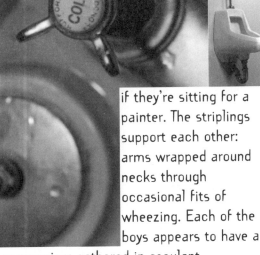

if they're sitting for a painter. The striplings support each other: arms wrapped around necks through occasional fits of wheezing. Each of the boys appears to have a companion; gathered in osculant, whispering clusters they look over each other with the scrutiny of surgeons. Couples nonchalantly twist their partners' curls around their fingers, or fiddle with the elastic of their pants.

They compare body parts, from navels which they finger, to genitals which are delicately handled like apricots.

Once in a while there is a confusion of shrieks and yells. I've never seen what sets them off, but the noise draws me over. The clamour of faces and torsos piled up on the floor is a little perturbing. There is no way of telling whether they're contorted in combat or embroiled in entertainment. They squeeze one another with the passion of pirates, and leave grinning teeth-marks on each other's thighs; lips clamped to flesh like limpets, enticing mauve bruises to emerge.

When they are all exhausted and untangled they slowly disband; partners appear to have been misplaced in the pandemonium but the older boys soon start to peruse for a potential new confidant. Messages pass with nothing more than a flutter of lashes; signals are understood. The new comrades acknowledge each other with a nod, then consolidate in corners.

Swimming Pool Girls are less fickle and haphazard with their friendships but when they fall out the rift can last an age and the pool comes close to overflowing with all the salty sentiment.

A few of us belong to The Five Metre Club, a select group who have penetrated the myths of The Deep End and overcome the terror of The Diving Board.

The air is thin at the summit. Our goggles cloud over as we slither along the length of the narrow plank. The horde of squealing Shallow End Girls nibble on polystyrene floats as they watch us grip onto the edge with just our toes. Coquettishly we raise our arms then somersault into the depths

— and from that distance they can't see we've screwed up our eyes.

There is a momentary hush as everyone waits for us to surface.

The 5m gang do nothing but perpetuate the mysteries of that part of the pool where your feet can't reach the bottom; emerging with tales of opaque octopi and diaphanous jellyfish. Triumphantly we paddle back, holding keys and coins between our teeth; by the time we reach the shallows we resemble ships encrusted with barnacles as inquisitive winged water-babies cling onto our backs.

After these intrepid voyages we get priority over The Underwaterfall. The pressure of the warm surge gushing out from the floor feels almost solid; forceful enough to keep two afloat.

We lie on our backs, our heads interlocked, resting on each other's bony collars, arms outstretched and entwined. Rolling our tongues inside our mouths to form gobstoppers, we push them against one another's cheek. You can also enfold your legs around your companion's waist, stomachs held close, and sail the heaving swell trying to break you apart.

As a Swimming Pool Girl you are susceptible to bouts of agitation; I envy the intimacy of The Changing Rooms where pleasures can go unnoticed. This nervous disposition — only made worse by the temperature — arises at the thought of The Underwater Viewing Gallery. Periodically, beams of bleached-out light illuminate the bathers and we spy distorted figures peering through the pool's one glass wall. Our home transforms into a public aquarium. This is where adults can get a glimpse into our queendom; where grown-up men spend asphyxiated evenings pressed against perspex.

If our games are interrupted we all hook our feet under the metal handrail and gaze up at the ceiling, counting stars in protest, and their necks crane to view the rows

of derrieres hovering below the surface. Ingenuous infants who grow bored take the opportunity to perform tightly choreographed, synchronised routines; and lap up muted applause. The 5m gang can hold their breath the longest; we push our noses up the glass and pull grotesque expressions. Sometimes, to blur their vision, we produce clouds of foggy urine right before their eyes and besides, we enjoy the warm sensation that filters through our suits.

Peeing in The Pool is usually prohibited.
Screaming in The Shallows is supposed to be suppressed.
Fondling in The Foot-bath, forever, will be forbidden.
And desire in The Deepend is diffidently denied.

But that hasn't discouraged me yet.
I love my saliferous sisters and couldn't leave them if I tried; my body is no longer suited to an outside, arid existence. But recently, when all the girls have drifted out to sleep, their heads resting on undulating floats, I plunge noiselessly into the fathoms: I breathe. My lungs shut down. The water caresses as it pours through my gills. With arms at my sides and legs close together, I move as an eel.

A Seahorse instructs me in the art of swimming upright. He hooks me like a fish — his tail between my legs — I feel the muscles down his back contract against my belly; it tickles, and we somersault, swimersault, over and over till I turn the colours of bladderwrack.

Mostly I spend these nocturnal voyages alone: surveying my self; peeling away leaves of skin spliced to my bathing costume. You see, it feels like two baby sea anemones are lodged inside my chest. I scratch away at my scales, trying to uncover treasures: searching for the funny-bone which convulses between my thighs when The Seahorse nets me.

My friends in The 5m Club haven't realised it but I've been feigning my audacity. I can sense it draining away — and I'm learning to blush. I'm starting to understand the fascinations of The Underwater Viewing Gallery.

Those aged, fixated faces slowly dissolve as their clammy breath fogs the spectacle — are they pressing themselves close to the protective perspex as I do against the porthole in that door?

I appreciate that the Changing Room Boys' lavatorial behaviour seems somewhat facile; forever reaching into their pants with access in the front, relentlessly tugging the withered hides around each other's members till they glisten. Weeing away the hours.

Swimming Pool Girls have their pastimes too, but why do I want to get caught up in Changing Room clamours, wearing only their bruises of affection, emerging smelling of Sultry and sticky with saliva from their snail-like tongues?

I have been a child forever and there are things I have to know.

cough syrup

5

The pavement rough and grey against my face and my shoes filling up with blood. After a bit when things have calmed down some, John Paul picks me up. The glass from the chip shop window makes a noise under the soles of cheap shoes and I'm still trying to get my head back after having it kicked in.

I don't exist, I'm not real for the next eight hours. I'm on office-time, underwater, everything frozen by boredom. A few people mention my face but they don't really care. Pilgrim checks the handbook to see if she can sack me for having facial lacerations first thing in the morning. All that ginger hair just fucking hating me, so I have a cup of tea and a fag while looking at the carpark spaces and thinking about Meg's arse. I adjust my hard-on straight away before anyone comes into the Smoking Room — don't want to be seen messing with it if one of the typists arrives with a Silk Cut under bad mascara and limp hair. Jack comes in and winces at my face; all red and bumpy, it looks worse than it feels.

"You don't look the kind who reads Kerouac and worries about stuff," he says, picking out bits of tobacco from the end of a roll-up.

I should be able to fix cars like Dad or rewire houses like Billy Junior, but I can't do any of those useful things. All I want to do is write books about Meg, who says I'll have to change my name to get published because I sound like an idiot at the minute. But I can't really change it — she might have but it's different for me — all I've ever been told is that people like me have to settle for what we've got.

3

It's not something I feel good about doing, but when I can't sleep and I'm covered with the familiar bedroom darkness and all I can think about is wanting to shag Meg, then it's hard for me to leave it inside of my pants. I feel fucking awful afterwards when I'm mopping it up with toilet paper — I feel about as horny as cough syrup.

2

I get into work, another day of holding my breath. Today will be like yesterday no matter how hard I try to paint a difference onto its hours. It's an English story: not trying hard enough at school, wanting to shag Justine from Elastica, ending up here moving paper and going barmy with it. The only thing worse than drowning in this Civil Service bath is succeeding.

Pilgrim is watching me doing nothing — it makes her angry that I don't mind my hands being empty; she thinks my head is too (anaemic ginger whelk on my back all day). Jack and me both want away from this, but he can't afford to be out of work and I've nothing else to do when Meg's not around.

1

Throwing up my daft belly in the toilet I hope nobody important is sitting trousers around their ankles in the next cubicle listening to the stains of last night. I grope for the handle and flush with my head still a little in the bowl, feel a slight spray of water and pretend I'm at the seaside. In the mirror my hair is all over. Splashes of sick fleck the top of my teeshirt making the logo hard to read. If I can't see much when I take another shy look in the mirror it's because I'm fading: soon there won't even be a white face with a bit of acne here — just a pair of clean pants and some dirty jeans on the floor.

kevin lloyd

iTs QUIET out here   juST me & SPACe
...ENDless SPaCE

of cOUrse i menDED the PUMP [PPs234/38/ra98]
hours^2 ago!!

took ME ...er... 5m 32s   hardLY NEEDed mending reaLLY

just a TWEAK from a WREnch

BUT i haD to GEt away from THEM for a FEW houRS

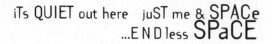

IRREGULAR ORBIT

MATTHEW ASTROP

its so NICE out HEre   just
STARgazing & floatING

PERfect peace & QUIET
a a a H H !

BETter tuRN the INTERcom on   ...sEE what THEYre ᵘᵖ TO   ...see
IF im wanTED
-click-
        Remould, you fucking cocksucker...
                                -click-
DEAR me   the LANGuage thESE huMANs *use!*   these WORDS are
all MaRKED *** IN my DICTIONary = DANGER!   EXTreme cauTION
IMpolite & offENSIVE languAGE
-click-
        Come in!   You useless cunt...
                        -click-
ThaTs PETER   APPARENTLY a SOFTware ENGIneer   he mustVE
LIED about his QUALIficatioNS to get ON this SHIP   he KNows
NOTHing
-click-
        iM here   iVE nearLY fixed the PUMP
                                -click-
-click-
        Look here...
a woMANs voice   thaTs JOSIE   pretty muCH *IN CHARGE* since
Captain HAYNES died   Captain HAYNES was OK²   SHE WAS gOd
TO ME   ...i Mean GOOD to me

...you've been out there for four sodding hours, I'd suspect you were wanking only I know your lot can't...

a LOT of laughter FROM the other CREW membeRS at that BON MOT

...you've had your intercom off, which you are not, repeat not, fucking well allowed to do ...stop pissing about at the end of that fucking lifeline and come in!
                              -click-
...YOU see THEY TALK to me AS if i DONt matTER ITs because iM not huMAN

well iVE had enough   HA!   theyRE NOT going to PUSH remould [OH that STUpid name] around ANY MORE
-click-
        JOSIE iM NOT coming IN until you TALK TO me POLITELy
                                                          -click-
-click-
    Fuck you!
            -click-
-click-
    all i WANT is for YOU to APOLOgise
                                    -click-
-click-
    Stuff it up your arse...

charmING

                        ...come in in ten minutes or we'll cut off
    your air supply, you spineless prick.
                              -click-
dEAR me

THis LOT are ENGLISH   quite the WORST to work for
APPARENTly 400 years AGO they haD an EMPIRE & used to RUN
most of EARTH!
inCREDible   isnT IT?   ???
i WOULDnt trust THIS loT to make a CHEESEBuRGER
LOOK what HAPpened to Captain HAYNES...

EXPLANation: 1 of THEM — PHIL —
              had the job OF cleanING the FOOD processing UNITs
              FILtraTION plant [a TYPE 552/hj845.76]
it ONLY had To bE done 4x a YEAR   but HE couldNT bE BOTHERed
HE used to GO DOWn to THe plant   turn ON the HOSES
so EVERYone could heAR them runNING
but INSTEAD of cleanING the grilles
HEd sit there READING comix & CHEWing gum
Well...   ALL sorts of BACteriA festered THERE
UNTil a batch of CHEESEBuRGERS got INfected
JANE   ...sorry... Captain HAYNES ate ONE   got INfected & DIed

                thAT was 3 yeARs AGO

my EXISTence has been HELL since

ALL THEY do ALL day LONG
                        is laZe about
THEY driNK lager & smoke someTHING very smelly that THEY grow
in the HYDROponics uNIT

dirty PLATEs & disheS   left EVERYwhere
dirty CLOTHES   ditto

THEY pair OFF & have SEXual interCOURSE   whenEVER THEY feel
like IT
THIS is AGAINST reguLAtions

some of the women have even exposed themselves to me
& taunted me about my lack of sex drive
i CANnot facE them anyMORE   i wonT take *ANY* more BULLYing
remould HAS HAD ENOUGH
-*click*-

    Look, you spastic!   We're going to cut off your airline and the
    power if you don't come in.

                                -*click*-
iM not ANSWERing
-*click*-

      I'm not joking, dick brain.

                              -*click*-
THEY taunt me BEcause THEY canT staND EACH other
-*click*-

    Remould, how the fuck will you survive?

                              -*click*-
HOw will THEY survive WITHout me?

iM the ONLY one who REMEMbers to RESET the CO_2 filter ON the
AIR recirculator
             in FACT   i THINK iM the ONLY one who knows HOW
same thing FOR WATER   they all URINATE in the shower facility
WHAT do THEY think THEY drink?
it DOESnt rain in SPACE   OR haveNT they NOticed
humans...   YUK2!!
iD RATHer die than LIve with THEM

iF i MANOEUVRE myself A bIT   iCAN see INside
THEYre arguING   JOSIE & PETER
iCAN see JOSIE reach for tHE interCOM
-*click*-

    That's it — if you don't come inside right now, we're cutting
    you off.

      -*click*-

SHE looks UP   HER eyes meET mine
-*click*-
   Are you coming in?
                -*click*-
SHE looks SPITEful & petuLANT   i SHAKe my HEAD slowly
SHE turns AWAY FRoM me   & SPeAKs to PETER
HE smileS & punches A few BUTTons

there IS a smaLL exploSION in my CHest
the AIR hose SNAPs away   TWISTing like a SNaKE
a RUSHing soUNd   i CAn feel AIR escAPing

my BOdy feels wEAk
& i CAN no lonGER move my ARMS & LeGS
the POWER line is PULLed out
my THOUght processes   SLOW   down   ....

i   AM   driFTiNG now   & WINDing DOWN
LOOKing at THE great SILVER bulk of THe shIP
itS beginNING to PULL away
leaviNG me ALONe in SPaCE

not TO worry
a COUPLe of ADJUSTments
                & my SOLAR panels UNfold
THe SURGE of poWER feels good
CHECK SYSTEMS...

all OK

Dyou KNOW?
        i THiNK THEY really thought i WAS a BIO-being LIKE them
ha ha ha
manKIND madE me to SERVe manKIND   but no more

iD reaLLY like TO meet my MAKER 1 day

if ONLY to find oUT how s/he CoULD BElong to the SAME SPeCIES
as that LOT?
my MAKER creaTED me
while THEIR finest hour WAS the ABILity to BELCH in time
                                to the THUNDERBIRDS THeme music
THATs 1 deliGHT iLL never HAVE to experiENCE aGAIN
wheeee!!   freedom

my CPU is estiMATED TO LaST...
1000^2 years
& thereS no RuST in SPACE
i MIGHT find a PLACE with an ATMOSphere
& be ABLE to use MY PNEUmatic limBS again
but if not   SO WHAT

now THEN   look ARound me
calCULATE the STars   GOOD...
A short BURst of ROCKET power
& off OLD remould GOES   on an IRREGular ORbit
for ever   into space
perfect peaceful space   AMEN

BROKEN PARABLES
REUBEN LANE

Lift the teapot down
from the shelf.

A rope of hemp. A skein of silk.

Take the lid off.

He asks — "What's so wicked
about a pile of money and a
crate of vodka?" But then
someone had warned me — "Don't
listen to him — he talks a crock
of shit." It was in this big
house — something from the 60's
— all wood floorboards — white
walls — and then this one room —
the whole of the back of the
house — a swimming pool down one
end and at the other a marble
floor where loads of people were
dancing. And a balcony
overlooking it.

Turn the tap on. Run water into the pot. Swill around and empty.

Waves of air – hot air from the bakery underground – out through the vent. A woman with no teeth lies sleeping on the pavement wrapped in cardboard and plastic.

    The bread and rolls baking – the pastries – the doughnuts fried – the can of strawberry jam – the confectioner's custard. She wakes with a wet mouth – dribble drying on her lips. The rattle of tin trays – the crash of an oven door opening and shutting – the loaves and cakes dashed out and knifed onto the counter. The slam of the flour dredger. The wooden crates pulleyed up to the shop – the rustle of greaseproof paper.

Put the teapot down on the table.

"Put them away for Christmas – Medium; Large and Extra Large."

    "Fresh bananas. Fresh satsumas."

    "Before we go – eh?"

    "Well – at least it never rained – And 'nuf said."

    "A catalogue for some soft gay porn? Or the greatest video hits of 'Take That'?"

    "I was looking forward to this Autumn – but it hasn't really delivered the goods. Somewhere on the calm side of miraculous."

Dodgy merchandise – knocked together in some factory out in Essex. Take your own advice – Sometimes it's just a case of riding it – watching the clock change – feeding times and in between. Drying your gloves over the stove.

Switch the kettle on at the socket.

The night before – the bride-to-be helps her mum bake some figs in the oven. They slice them open – smear them with honey – cook them again and serve them on a glass plate with vanilla ice cream.

And everybody comes to the wedding and the reception afterwards. They all wear paper hats and bung streamers and step out to the band. No expense spared. A three tiered wedding cake. A limousine to the hotel. The floor in the bedroom rocking. The bouncy bed. The tip for the bell boy. The golden taps in the bathroom. The marbled blue tablet of soap. The tears in the mirror. The fat hand turning off the bedside lamp.

Open the lid of the cardboard box. Count out two tea bags and drop them into the pot.

She descends the stairs that lead to the chamber where they'll strap her into a chair – a cord of electricity tied to a

leather cap crushing down her hair. And the
throw of a switch — frazzle and smoke.
Always a few spectators — and the doctor
to check she's really dead.
    'Cos Jesus makes her laugh.
    And she could have danced on the
bedstead. In her night-gown and the light
of the Mexican moon.

Take a mug from the drying-up rack.

Venturing. Scouting. Coins and ceiling wax.
Slim boys with ribs and hips. And they
grab them as they go by. The horses on the
carousel. The driver on the Ghost Train. It
should only take me twenty five minutes by
bike — We'll meet outside the club — hey?
    I am an escapologist — escaping from one
shove and tumble into a jam packed tube
train — stuck between stations on the
hottest day of the year.

Tip and pour an inch of milk into the bottom of the mug.

Dripping wet — Run — hide — quick — put
clothes on — pants inside out. Laughing.
Yelling. Wet feet slapping out of the
showers. Rummaging in my Adidas bag — the
stink of unwashed sports kit — stuff it
inside. Boys surrounding me. Towels wrapped
around their waists. Wet towels. Trousers —
A shirt button snaps off — Socks — Where

are my socks? Looking at the floor — eyes to the ground. No words. Just get out of here. The chlorine from the swimming pool. It'll be getting dark outside. Do I need to go to the classroom first? — Books for homework. Maths. Equations. Logarithms. Mr Banson will come up to my desk tomorrow and peer at me — stop for an hour — and tell me I'm like a baboon because I scratch my armpit. Shame — they'll never shut up about it — They'll taunt me — call me names — tell the girls and they'll be even worse because they're so clever. And I'll try to explain — it was the water — not because of those football bodies swishing the mud off — my mind romping between them — turning cartwheels in the steam hot showers.

In Monument Valley the cowboys roam and the Apaches wait on the brow of the hill — ready to ambush them.

Guys I know go out cruising on the Heath. That anonymous sex — where you don't talk to each other — don't even tell each other your name. Just light a cigarette and browse at what's on offer. Even in the Winter — Chuck your coat on the ground — or just go down on them — your knees cushioned by the crinkly leaves.

Wait for the kettle to boil.

Ethan rang me up out of the blue. Said
"I'm in London. Can I come and talk to
you?" - I said "Sure" - "When?" - "How
about now?" I said - "Well" - "I'm going
over to my folks' house - pick up some
books and stuff - they're not there. If
you want you could meet me there. I could
raid the freezer - Cook us up some lunch."
He said "That'd be fine." - "A couple of
hours?" - "I'll ring you from the station."

I cycled to South London - Chucked some
clothes in the washing machine and switched
the heating up - remembering how he liked
it hot. The phone rang: "I'm just catching
the train from Victoria - I'll see you
down there in twenty minutes." And there he
was in his green jacket - carrying a
couple of carrier bags and his brown
leather satchel.

I looked him over to see if I could
spot any changes. A bit plumper maybe -
the remnants of a South of France out in
the fresh air tan.

This turned out to be all about him -
and the state he's in. He smoked a quick
rollup as we walked up the hill to the
house. We sat in the kitchen and I asked
him about his stay in France. Out in the
country near Toulouse - minding a house -
doing the garden. Which is when he said to
me - "Oh Rooley - I completely lost it out
there." - "What do you mean?" - "My head.
They took me into hospital for a couple of
days. Pumped me up with valium. I couldn't

clear my thoughts — like the things I
could do — I could never get to sleep —
I'd listen to the World Service and then
about 2 o'clock I would blank out — like I
was a psychopath. All the bad things — the
evil inside of me — No telling what I
might do."

And his head began to nod back and
forward — like a nervous tic. At first I
wasn't sure I wasn't imagining it. I stared
at him.

He stopped and searched in his bag.
"I don't usually take these during the day
— but I think I'll have one now — Don't
be scared" — as he gulped down a white
shiny pill.

"So what are you going to do now Ethan?
Where you going to live?" — "I think I'll
do this play. It's all custard pies — a
kids' show for Christmas — I don't want to
do it — but they asked me — and I want to
be with people."

But no — "What about treatment? Don't
you want to find out what's wrong?" —
"It's psychological — they've done tests.
I've got to get me a place to live —
somewhere I can stay for a bit — some calm
— some rest — Get myself a GP — get
referred — it all takes time." "But Ethan"
I want to yell at him — "Letting yourself
be stuffed with tranquillisers — hitching
round the country — looking for some peace
— contradicting yourself every five
minutes." — "I went to Norfolk when I

first got back. I must have been there a
week – but I've had amnesia – I can't
remember anything – it's embarrassing – I
was talking to my nephew and I said 'Heck
– I'd really like to see that movie The
Fugitive' – and he said 'Yeah – but Ethan
we went to see that just the other week
when you were down here.'"

The pill works – he stops shaking. And
knowing I mean something to him – whatever
– that he'll at least listen to my advice
– I grab him by the shoulders – and say
"Come on Ethan – You've got to go and get
help – like now – tomorrow morning."

Ice and snow. The yellow twizzle of the
gritting lorry trying to climb the hill –
Sprinkling out salt and sand.

Allow two minutes to brew.

We carry Ethan's stuff across London on the
tube – a word processor; a duvet; a
rucksack of clothes; his satchel; a
holdall. On TV Jamie Bulger's parents tell
their story EXCLUSIVELY in the News Of The
World. Scoop. Order your copy now. Which
cracks him up. His new room. A security
television link; so when you ring the front
doorbell you're lit up for the camera. And
there's spunk stains on the carpet. "I'll
ring you when I get back home." I am a
superhero in my cape and balaclava – except
no one recognises me – they try and shoot

me down and paste up pictures of me with
black caption bold letters 'WANTED FOR
MURDER'. I am innocent. I put my arms
around Ethan and pull him into my chest.

I want some paint so I can spray the
sky sienna red. It's not good fortune - or
just rewards - or a little bit of heaven -
or a tad of Utopia - or the freefall of
love - or the whereabouts of sussing it
out; it's just me - on my own - stringing
it together and moving on and stirring and
splashing the water - so I can never see a
clear reflection of what's ahead or what
lay behind - except here - tap it - in my
angelic head.

Pour the steaming tea from the pot into the mug.

A voice cries out in the wilderness. A
hollow throat - the tongue cut and sore
with gangrene. A straight road. A woman on
the pavement who for a copper coin will
rub your feet with oil and dry them with
the long tresses of her white hair. The
booth where they'll try and sell you a
lottery ticket. The trays of syrup muffins
and cream cheese bagels. The children with
their spinning tops - the adolescents with
their counterfeit Kalashnikovs.

A bus ride to the prophet. A carpark
and roadside caravan cafe selling hot dogs
and Coca Cola. People with missing limbs
crouch in the sand - a crutch and a

begging bowl lying at their feet — their
stumps swathed in grubby bandages.

And the voice of the prophet is
broadcast over the PA. He stands on a
podium behind bulletproof glass. To see
better you can hire a pair of binoculars.
He announces how he has been living out
here in the wilderness — wearing only a
smock of camel's hair and eating nothing
but locusts and wild honey.

The crowd groans sympathetically. "But
after me" he says "there will come a
greater man — the latchet of whose shoes I
will not even be worthy enough to stoop
down and undo. In a moment I will baptise
those of you who choose — here in the
river — with water. But this man — he will
baptise you with the Spirit of God."

The sandwich board man stands outside the
Trocadero.

He shouted at me — screamed at me to stand
against the wall. And he tugged down my
jeans so they were hanging about my ankles.
And then he stood behind me — and pressed
himself up against me — pushing me hard
into the wall. His hands snuck under the
elastic of my shorts.

"How's this for you?"

"Sorry — Look I've..."

"Sure you're not? — Go on — say it —
say this doesn't do nothing for you."

Drink your tea. Mind the leaves at the bottom.

The way – forward. The ribbon highway. The golden path. The burning torches. The light of the moon. And heaven is draped in banners of greens and purples – lanterns hanging – stubs of fat candles. A big ledger to write your name in – the extent of your ambitions – the amount of time you'll be willing to listen to others – to counsel them – to guide them on their way. The fight against demons; the tubes of tranquillisers; the modern addiction of waiting – hurting so hard for something – like a job or love to fill the void.

Bringing grapes to the patient in hospital. The fortune cookies. The bunches of daffodils. Aching to be good – but so clumsy at it – and nowadays so unsure what 'good' is anyway.

But listen up – under the loud thud of your heartbeat – alone in a landscape – your eyes alight on a scene that brings you a snatch of bliss. Depending on only you and the real world – not the flesh and blood of other people – but the grass beneath your belly – the waves breaking in you ears – the salt on your tongue – the wind buffeting your face. And perhaps this is the very single reason we go on – to find this again and again – in some other place – on the plains of a desert; from the peak of a snowcapped mountain; way

beneath at the bottom of the sea with the shoals of red and yellow fish and the tentacles of the octopus. Or closer to home – in some ramshackle graveyard – or taking shelter from the drizzle in a cave on the moors.

Sometimes it is heroic just to bunk up and over the wall separating one day from the next. The little magic of survival. The big magic of taking part. Catching the train out of here – never quite knowing who you are.

UNPUTDOWNABLE

nick rogers

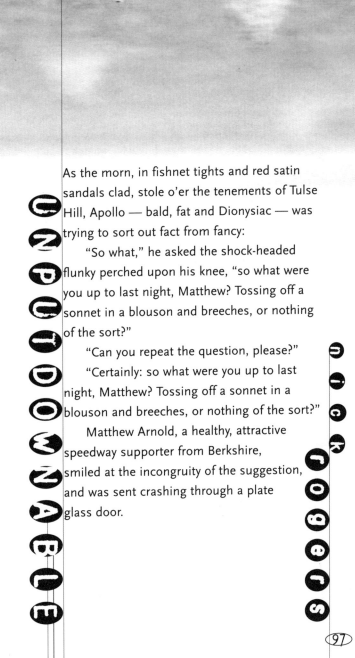

As the morn, in fishnet tights and red satin sandals clad, stole o'er the tenements of Tulse Hill, Apollo — bald, fat and Dionysiac — was trying to sort out fact from fancy:

"So what," he asked the shock-headed flunky perched upon his knee, "so what were you up to last night, Matthew? Tossing off a sonnet in a blouson and breeches, or nothing of the sort?"

"Can you repeat the question, please?"

"Certainly: so what were you up to last night, Matthew? Tossing off a sonnet in a blouson and breeches, or nothing of the sort?"

Matthew Arnold, a healthy, attractive speedway supporter from Berkshire, smiled at the incongruity of the suggestion, and was sent crashing through a plate glass door.

A beautiful-ankled quantity surveyor, 29, was performing a pirouette on the gravel drive. She helped Matthew to his feet, put her hands on his shoulders, and marched the Reading-born Bradford fan back inside. A queer smile spread over Apollo's face.

"You have amused me, Matthew, and will not be punished. No, you will make me breakfast."

"Sure," said Matthew. "Frosties?"

Matt's audacity earned him ten days' leave......Meanwhile, in the heart of Dalston, a hooded sybil sat down to write a letter.

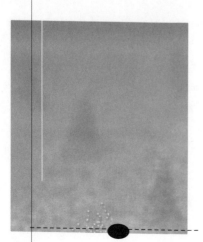

The fifth and final draft read as follows:

The Misericord,
Islington Borders
October, 19, 199-

Dear Miss Stiff,

Thank you for the tape and the winding sheet. It's definitely a lead but the message of malaise, I'm afraid, is a bluff. She talks too fast.

The transcript requires the following amendments. I can't say I'm sorry. What do you live off? An embarras de richess?

Line 4: 'If you haven't got the legs you've got to have the brains', should read: 'I bet she never asked a boy out in her life'.

Line 9: delete.

Line 19: 'Pervert not truth', should read: 'Herring, bin bags, double cream'.

Thanks.

Note: a nice nihilist wouldn't have written a word.

I will see you next Tuesday. Bring thing and Burke's A Grammar of Motives. Till then, dress plain and follow orders. Only two weeks to go.

Vinnie

And keep ear tagging those calves!

III

As chance would have it, at the same time as Lavinia sealed the letter, Grandma squirmed inimitably in her seat in Stockwell... At thirty-six and over six feet tall, the lone mother-of-two had just published her first novel: a *roman fleuve* of goose-pimpling timelessness, entitled *Royal Gardening Nazi Pussy*. Sitting opposite Grandma in the brightly lit box room, Slasher McCloud – literary critic, philanderer and social reformer – lobbed the inert, bulky object into the bin. Grandma gave an old-fashioned look and cried:

"Ten years of toil, ten years of disciplined mental agony, went into the making of that—"

"Crock of shit."

Grandma smiled, stood up and sailed outside...

✪

It was a delightful evening, featuring a sky-blue sky with two pink, horizontal bands. Grandma hitched up her skirts and skipped down the street, singing Augustus Toplady's Rock of Ages. Then she pinned a man to the bonnet of an N-reg Audi.

"Nice car," purred Grandma, "wanna show me what it can do?"

"I can't drive," lied Matthew.

"I can," said Grandma.

✪

An hour later the Audi screeched to halt.

"I'm bored," muttered Matt.

"Me too," cried Grandma, slipping a C60 into the stereo, "isn't ennui absolutely enormous?"

"I can't remember. Where are we?"

"A remote country lane in Essex."

"Fucking brilliant."

"What?"

"*Snatch.*[1] Get going Grandma."

Grandma broke into a peal of refectory laughter, reversed the car and drove back to London.

✪

Matt kissed her goodbye—

"MWU!"

"UGH!"

—and watched the youngish novelist walk down the street...

[1] 'All I Want' / 'When I'm Bored' (Lighting Records, 1978)

She had excellent legs, the reviews were delusory[2], and Grandma was catapulted into mainstream chic.

IV

It was on the afternoon following the jaunt in the Audi that the door to Matt's bedroom groaned on its hinges. A slither of light fell across the floor.

"Who is it?"

"I'm not absolutely sure."

"M-M-Mrs Stiff!" stammered Matt; "I—I was just thinking about you."

"Ah, how sweet," she replied, slipping inside.

"I was having a wank."

"Passéist."

Passéist! At last, thought Matthew, a woman, who understands...

Mrs Stiff kicked the door to and flicked on the light. Her velvet shift dress was threadbare. Her black lace jacket was frayed at the collar. A coldsore was throbbing on her lip. She felt good.

"You look terrible," said Matthew.

"Thanks. Is there a back way out of here?"

"Yes. Show her out, Sasha."

The quantity surveyor slid out from under the quilt; Mrs. Stiff puckered her high, pale brow. The quantity surveyor showed her out.

✪

Sasha returned, clutching her ribs.

"What was that all about?" asked Matt, brave and unafraid.

"Anger, fear, quotation, denial, withdrawal."

"Glad to hear it."

[2]'Written in a language so pure and resonant it makes you sick' Maya Angelou; 'Awesomely ambitious, breathtakingly clever – like Dirty Weekend rewritten by Sir Walter Scott' Michael Winner; 'It happened because she was easy and weak' James Wood, in The Guardian; 'The book I've been waiting to read all my life' Rosemary West, in Durham Jail.

resenter

STEVE AYLETT

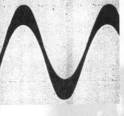 Everyone said I'd get a tumour the size of a barrage balloon if I didn't calm down. This would rupture a man like me in no time. Forgive and forget, they said, and were blank or angry when I asked how. Supposedly, other people kept their lower jaw behind the upper one without even thinking; they had a forehead strictly to keep their brain concealed, not as a screen on which to signal its bitter conclusions by a network of hammering veins. Reluctantly I conceded something had to be done.

I decided to store my resentment externally. Numbed myself with a twelve-gauge needle and teased out a group of nerves which stretched across the bedroom to a choline-rich nutrient tank—here their endings drifted like filamentous pondweed. Trepanning's for the birds, I thought, this'll release the whole nine yards and give it a home from home. Curb hate and fury into doubt and starvation—step up to the nineties.

Every night I'd rig up the nerve flex and settle to sleep, awakening refreshed and ready to confront another inferno of manipulation. I actually began to feel calmer and tentatively practised turning the other sunken cheek.

Third morning I found the nerve cable had detached and lay trailed along the floor—the other end was still immersed in the tank. I took to re-attaching the lead nightly to a wound I kept raw for the purpose and this arrangement was more convenient than before. Dreams of justice siphoned into the nutrient and marked their release by growing a bitter ball of tissue the size of an egg. Soon this elongated to form a frilled spinal ladder, which then fanned pale veins against the stained walls of the tank. These daily mutations were more fun to watch than the bleak-staring fish I used to incarcerate there.

As the aquarium clouded, my mood cleared. As it filled, I emptied. In fact I was becoming conveniently vapid. My friends'd see the change, I thought. It'd satisfy Suki and I'd be placid as the Dead Sea.

Suki was sat at the kitchen table reading the news aloud. Something had happened which had happened before and would again unless circumstances changed dramatically—but the paper quoted the shock of those unconnected with the event. Here were the press with money to earn and inflatable morals for emergencies and I didn't feel the slightest disgust or insult. 'Are you ill, sicko? I just said another guy went crazy and they're acting the same as last time, taking swift action with their gobs. So what's your view, genius? Where's all your opinions tonight?'

I took some milk out of the fridge. 'Oh, I'm sure they've got their reasons for doing sod-all, darling.'

'You said last time a total gun ban'd lose 'em a bunch of private donations.'

'Now why get so upset.'

'What about the paper here, shithead—totally inconsistent position from one day, one page to the next. What's the matter with you?'

'Yeah, terrible business isn't it.'

'Listen you moron, is this something to do with that neuron experiment in there?'

'You're smart—smarter than I am.'

In the bedroom the biomass had climbed the wall like a fungus, varicose channels reaching the ceiling.

At work my easygoing regimen bore hostile fruit: looks of bewilderment from those who had previously told me to cheer up under migraine strobes. Back home I walked into my room to find coral shelves of meat covering the walls and a pink tissue grid stretched like gum across the ceiling, an umbilical chandelier hanging from its centre. Cytoplasmic bulges pulsed and sweated. Even as I watched, dendrites were spreading like frost on a windshield.

Suki was appalled. 'What are you, nuts? A psycho? You think it's normal to have this much meat hung across the ceiling like streamers? Is it meant to be endearing? And what's this—codeine?'

I snatched the pills from her. 'For my nerves.'

'You can joke about this? Like everyone loops ganglion tissue over the lightshade this way? Look at that bladdersack in the corner, it's throbbing like a bastard.'

'I'm expressing myself, sweetheart, instead of bottling it up—I don't even need the synapse cable any more, that stuff knows what I'm thinking. You should be glad for me with this success here.'

'Success?' She kicked a protuberance, which burst. 'Is this blood? This is disgusting, I've had it.' And she slammed out of the flat.

I was so passive I took down a book at random and opened it onto this: 'When anyone offends against another, life is directed to compromise while creating an unperishable by-product. It's neither acknowledged nor eliminated—it's the nuclear stuff of justifiable revolt.' A tremor flubbered through the meat lattice as I thought about it. When the hell would a book offer advice that could actually be applied?

Next day I was fired for calling the boss 'Master'. ('Are you bored here?'/'Yes, Master.') When he said I was fired, I grinned out of politeness, thinking it was some ancient joke. I had a mouthful of coffee at the time and this cascaded onto a plug panel, shorting out the entire building. I felt okay about it but when I got home the flat was a steaming meat jungle; furniture hung from the swaying rind. As I hacked it down with a cleaver I thought positive—there's an upside to everything, and hopefully this wasn't it.

Examination of the matter revealed it was growing exponentially. Surely there was a cash-rich niche for this stuff. I took a few slabs of it onto the street. With all the marketing finesse of a gibbon I put up a placard saying Cheap Pullulating Guts and thought kids would snap it up like the Slime I'd enjoyed eating at their age. Instead I was threatened with arrest by some moron who thought his hat was fooling anyone about how tall he was.

Apparently you needed a license to sell undifferentiated tissue round here and there weren't any signs making the point.

'You won't have a height problem with these little beauties under your hat, I'm telling you.'

But he explained that though ignorance of the law was no defence, whirling violence was frowned upon also—it seemed I was obliged to help him pretend this was a fair fight.

'Suppose it won't be impossible to hunt down and memorise the hundred wads of statute hitting the list every week,' I remarked calmly. But the muscle flanges on my sales cart had liquidised and run together like boiling fat, forming a likeness of my own face contorted with rage. This veined bonce began bulging out of size and bellowing scorched-earth common sense at the copper and the world at large. The Bill's trousers crowded with whatever he used for brains and as he ran shrieking, the blathering matter flipped to the ground and panned out, flapping toward a drain like a beached ray. Liquefying, it slipped between the drain bars and disappeared. So much for the free market.

Outside my place, I saw that the building had cracked down the front and was leaking dendritic sludge like lava. A car was buoyed up and slowly overturned, windows popping. A manhole cover sprung and fat-striped nerve matter pushed from beneath like overflowing dough. This reared up and formed a giant mouth which yelled about the unavoidable presence of pasta in every single London meal. How much more complicated life is than Dante's *Inferno* would have us believe.

Took a thoughtful walk through the city, the earth rumbling around me. What I had here was an attitude problem—I shouldn't have it in me and I shouldn't let it out. That amounted to a requirement to deny my own existence as a feeling entity. After all, I'm young, male, white, English—the skill should be in my blood. We lead the world in denial and here I am wrecking the facade by knowing it.

The street heaved, buckling. A massive grudge broke the surface like the back of a whale. I hurried on, trying not to think anything bad about this bloody dove-grey decade. Passed the Revenue office and thought of the forty-two million quid spent proving that hot dry rocks can't produce cheap electricity. Passed a drug clinic and thought of the cabinet minister blithely addicted to cocaine. Passed a church and thought of someone dying for me without asking first. Passed a court where factual reality went to die. And I really felt nothing.

But the buildings were rupturing, knocked outward by the flowering matter of an abscess. TV news in a store window showed indistinct mayhem as nerves of dissent crisscrossed the city like telephone wires. A newsreader expressed genuine perplexity. This was understandable. I walked away and the store exploded in a gush of cerebral slime. There's a difference between getting it out of your system and getting your system out. The difference is acknowledgement of ownership and a tendency to brag.

I began kidding myself I could dispose of it the modern way. A formal complaint. I strode toward Parliament, then started to run—the rage rushed under the street behind me, flipping the pavement like dominoes.

Tie adjusted, name-badge discreetly straightened, I am physically and psychically preparing myself to serve the customer who is about to enter the shop. I slip my sleek, lightweight Kokia 3010 Hand Portable (recently bought to replace the somewhat primitive company issue TS900) back into the staticky confines of my trouser pocket and slide along the orange PlastiCovered sales counter

Ainsley John Roberts to a recessed computer console.

SHOP TALK

I begin busily key-tapping, thus presenting to the potential customer an image of conscientious efficiency (although in fact the computer is turned off). Staring absently at the dust-specked VDU I suddenly realise that I'm frowning and quickly relax my face into a placid smile. Three seconds after the door-chime sounds (a digitally sampled dial-tone) I stop tapping and look up, in order to acknowledge and evaluate the customer.

My three years' experience in the retail industry has equipped me with a finely-tuned evaluation system, not dissimilar in function to the orange PlastiCovered Questionnaire console, called "Tippsy", which stands beside the sales counter (with touch-sensitive screen, user-friendly display and extensive CD-ROM database). Based on criteria such as clothing, physiognomy, accent and general deportment, I can automatically calculate the class, occupation and hence the probable needs, desires and credit rating of any given customer.

In the moment it takes me to establish eye contact and execute the standard acknowledgement (a curt yet informal nod), I register: oversized woollen beanie half-hiding sharp pale junkie face (age indeterminate); scrawny neck thrusting from shabby hooded top; baggy torn-off jeans curtaining battered skate pumps. The overall effect places this yob firmly in the Unlikely Customer category.

I don't return my attention to the computer screen.

Undeterred, the yob silently slouches across the stylish yet durable carpeting (aqua with orange fleck) towards the main display, where the executive phones recline smugly in their glass-fronted cabinets. He scans the display, his sunken eyes

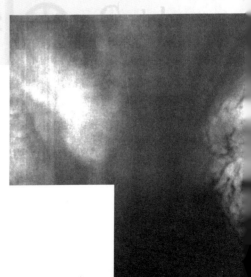

defacing each orange PlastiCovered shelf of elegant, compact portables with the coarse graffiti of his ghetto-bred ignorance. As he sneers up at the life-sized posters depicting the latest attractive models caressing the latest attractive models, I notice a length of phone-cable coiling out of his jeans pocket, the end severed.

It is situations like this which make me wish I'd stayed in catering.

As I deliberate the ethical/logistical viability of chucking him out and closing early, I imagine the obnoxious tone of Mr Taylor, the regional manager, crackling out of my Kokia (as it has done several times already today), rabbiting on about Declining Sales Figures, Competitive Marketing and Employee Commitment. Reluctantly, I move out from behind the sales counter.

The yob fixes his aerosol gaze on me as I glide towards him on autopilot, my mind casting about for the appropriate form of address. I opt for my own personalised variation on that standard retail idiom, the Inquiry Necessitating a Positive Response; delivery informal, casual even; with just a hint a condescension:

"You all right there, mate?"

My judicious use of protocol seems lost on the yob, however; he remains silently aloof. I reach the display and resignedly launch into the usual spiel.

"Ah, I see you're interested in the Manasonic M4000 there. A very popular model. Robust, reliable, easy to use; some very impressive features. Outclassed only, in fact, by the Crony CR-DX2000 and Kokia 3000 series, which offer similar features with enhanced battery performance..."

Alternating my attention between the executive phones and the hooligan's face, I become increasingly aware of an incompatibility of features, and begin to usher him physically across the shop while jargonizing on the relative merits of digital and (cheaper) analogue portables.

Having reached the smaller analogue display, I surprise myself by pitching headlong into what is effectively a eulogy on the joys of mass communication; my forced enthusiasm, spurred on somehow by the yob's mute impassivity, snowballs with every syllable.

"Contrary to much of the bad press it has been receiving, the Communications Revolution is about connecting people; Networking, in fact. You're never alone with a mobile phone... and as the man on the television says, 'It's Good to Talk!'..."

My oratory becomes more and more fervent and arbitrary, until one particularly graphic gesticulation dislodges the orange placard, bearing the company logo with the legend 'Talk is Cheap', from above the display. After pausing to realign the placard and regain something of my professional composure, I recommence the sermon.

"Here at The Talking Shop we believe that 'You Can't Overcommunicate'. Of course, many of our potential clients express concern about 'loss of privacy'; the harsh bleep of one's portable rending the otherwise harmonious atmosphere of a restaurant, health club... or crack den... resulting in acute irritation and embarrassment on the part of the user."

Pausing here, I worry that I may have overstated my case. The yob, who has until this point been staring intently at the chunky, lurid analogues, swivels his gaze back to me. Adopting a reassuring tone, I quickly resume: "...However, what such people regard as a possible loss of privacy, we like to call a gain in possibility. Like every other aspect of modern society, mobile phone ownership is about choice. After all," I add, smiling, "you can always turn it off."

At this point the discordant atmosphere is rent by the harsh bleep of my portable. Suppressing my acute irritation and embarrassment I mumble an "excuse me", raise the phone to my ear and, turning discreetly to face a wide double-glazed window, press the Receive button. (Click.) "Good afternoon, The Talking Shop, Barry speaking, how may I—"

"Barry?" The obnoxious tone of Mr Taylor, the regional manager, crackles out of my Kokia. "Barry! Well thank God!"

There is a wavering quality about his voice, which I put down to a bad connection; not an unusual occurrence.

"Mr. Taylor, can I call you back, I've got..."

"Barry! I'm at Kensington. All

sunset with an almost alien intensity.

A cursory scan informs me that no merchandise seems to be missing. As I relax and begin a proper stock-take there's another click from my Kokia, which is still clenched to my ear; this is followed immediately by a short burst of chaotic noise, then an ominous 'click... bzzz' as the line is cut off.

I'm halfway through keying in the Kensington number (I haven't yet got to grips with the One-Touch Speed-Dial function) when a surge of movement snags my attention. Looking up through the window I see a large crowd of people on the opposite side of the road. They are demolishing a privatised call-box with a varied arsenal of DIY and gardening implements.

A group of about a dozen of these maniacs then breaks off from the main crowd, gesturing towards my shop.

I shudder as if waking from a dream, and start frantically stabbing the 9 key on my Kokia. By now the group are halfway across the road. Panicking, I thrust the phone to my ear...

(Silence.)

our other branches are cut off. I've been trying them for the past fifteen minutes. I was beginning to think our whole network was down!"

This explains the wavering in Mr Taylor's voice; communication is his life. I offer to try the other branches on my Kokia but he interrupts again, his voice distorting into a panicked sing-song.

"Barry, there's a crowd of... people coming in. I'm putting you on hold."

Taking advantage of this temporary reprieve, I turn to apologise to my customer, who has vanished. I spin around, but see only empty blue floor-space and orange PlastiCovered shelves, glowing in the late afternoon

The questionnaire was on his lap. He was pulling back on the bulldog clip and letting it go, absently. He had a lot on his mind. The opposite sex, mainly. He had very little success with them, the opposite sex. On second thoughts, he had a great deal of success with the opposite sex, but only up to a point.

Iain Grant

A question of what, exactly?'

The fact that he still thought of them as the opposite sex was telling. They were different, women. Strange chaps, with their moods and their bodies. His mother had been a woman.

There was no sex, though. He was from Milngavie. His parents were still alive.

He'd left home and Glasgow at 21 with a head full of ambition on his shoulders, a rucksack on his back, a degree in journalism under his belt, and a world full of promise before him. He headed for Edinburgh for a change of scene and started going out with women seriously. This meant having a place of his own to bring them back to, and having the freedom to go back to their place when the occasion warranted it. He didn't altogether realise it, but he was rather attractive with his height and his chiselled features and his piercing blue eyes, and he had an air of confidence about him which many women found appealing. He was an old-

He got on with them well, a lot of the time. He went out with them, and enjoyed their company in social settings. It was when things became romantic that he got into hot water. Even then, he enjoyed the candlelit dinners, the music, the fragrances, the touching, the sweet nothings, the frolicking, the foreplay.

fashioned gentleman. He was waiting for the right girl to come along.

After a good few years of this, he found himself wanting to settle down. He began to look for a more long term relationship. What's more, he had physical urges, urges that he knew his mother wouldn't approve of, but which he realised were acceptable so long as they were directed towards the legitimate goal of the establishment of a family. He thought about trying to get a grip on himself, but realised that he'd

been doing that for far too long.

It wasn't that he was fussy. It was just that he was looking for... what, exactly?

Well, for the ideal girl, he supposed. If she existed. That was

the reason for the questionnaire. It was designed to identify the ideal girl in 20 easy steps. Seven and a half years, he'd been using it.

The questionnaire was administered thus: he would go out with a nice girl. They would have a romantic dinner or evening at the theatre or even, in summer, walk in the country. Then they would go back to his place, or hers, for a nightcap, and he would whip it out. The questionnaire. He would show it to her and say, nervously, 'Look, I really like you, and I'd like to get to know you a lot better, but I'd really appreciate it if you answered some questions before we take things any further.

It'll save a lot of time and inconvenience later.'

If she said yes, and a surprisingly high percentage of his companions did, he would read her the questions, marking off her have found charming at one stage of his life, when he was fifteen and had a taste for foolish pranks and loud trousers, but which was not a suitable character trait for the mother of his children. Of the 103

responses as she answered.

He was reading over the most recent version of the questionnaire now, thinking it over. Maybe it needed another tinkering with, or something.

> 1. Celtic or Rangers?
> (Celtic 0, Rangers 0, Neither 2)

This question was here to sort out the men from the boys from the word go. Football was his abiding hate. This was one of the few characteristics he was conscious of having inherited from his father. A liking for football was boring enough in men, but in girls it invariably went with a laddish irresponsibility which he might

replies he'd had to this question, only one had scored the full two points. Jenny, he remembered. Lovely girl, though he'd been rather baffled by her response to question 17. They'd shared a beautiful dinner and surprisingly powerful mutual lust, but her score had been only 86%. Although this was the highest anyone had ever scored, he was looking for something... more, and he really thought he should hang on until he got a score in the high nineties at least.

2. What do you have for weekday breakfast?
(Cereal 0, porridge 1, toast 2)

He'd never understood cornflakes. Even less so Weetabix. His mother had given him porridge most mornings, even in summer, but as an adult he'd grown to appreciate the lightness, convenience and adaptability, given the large number of toppings available, of toast. He was trying to break free of his heritage. He naturally assumed that his ideal mate would have similar jentacular appetites.

3. Tea or coffee?
(Tea 0, coffee 1, depends 2.)

He hated dogmatism, something to do, he reasoned, with his father's being a kirk elder and his life-long Unionism, and he'd come to the conclusion over the years that he hated it more in tea drinkers than in coffee drinkers. Why? He didn't know. It was a mystery, but some things you just have to take at face value.

4. Who makes you laugh?
(Laurel & Hardy, Eric & Ernie, Chic Murray, Tommy Cooper, early Goon Show etc 2)

Self-explanatory. Humour, he knew, was one of the ties that bind, being thicker than water. His parents had shared a taste in humour, one of the few things they'd had in common, and the main thrust of it had been to find almost everything unfunny. They despised everything he found amusing. He laughed,

they sniffed, he giggled, they pooh-poohed. His sister too. Tommy Cooper, Eric and Ernie, even Chic Murray.

she only read the women's page, so she didn't really count.

---

5. Which daily newspaper do you read? (Express/Mail 0, none/Sun/Mirror/Record 1, broadsheet (inc FT) 2)

This was not mere snobbery on his part. He'd observed over the years that, though he was capable of physical attraction to a reader of the so-called middle-brow tabloids, he found it impossible to hold conversations with them. This rendered them, to all intents and purposes, unattractive anyway. He'd found that there were people who read the other tabloids for fun, but on the whole he preferred broadsheet readers as they tended to be better informed. He had once had a horrendous experience with a Guardian reader, but he remembered her telling him that

---

6. Pepsi or Coke? (Pepsi 0, Coke 2)

He was sorry and all that, but he just didn't like Pepsi, even if he was sometimes convinced that the CocaCola Corp was a sinister organisation hell-bent on world domination. The potential for domestic disharmony caused by the presence in his fridge of the other variety of beverage was too horrific to contemplate. It would be his parents all over again with their Typhoo/Tetley's teabag disagreement and the Stork/Vitalite hostility which had lasted for more than ten of his formative years and had been pursued by both sides with a bitterness which, even now, many years later, caused him to shake his head in wonder.

---

7. List favourite spectator sports

This was one of his 'open' questions. He hadn't set prescribed values to any answers, being mainly on the lookout for football fans who slipped through

the net of question 1, tennis fans who would make his life a misery in June by watching Wimbledon on television, and those people who were, inexplicably, interested in golf. He wasn't quite sure how he'd react if he ever received a reply with cricket nominated, having never known anybody with a fondness for the game. He was willing to keep an open mind on the subject.

> 8. List food dislikes

Another open question. In his experience people were more likely to be bound together by the things they didn't like than by the things they did. If he'd ever had the answer 'eggs and peanuts' he would have made an immediate offer of marriage, but it had never arisen, though the two items had occurred separately. One respondent had said 'anything red', another had said simply 'vinegar' and several, far too many in his view, had ruled themselves right out by listing more than five items. He couldn't stand a fussy eater. He'd had enough of that with his sister. His other guiding principle here, of course, was no vegetarians.

> 9. Star sign?
> (Aries, Taurus, Gemini, Cancer, Leo, Sagittarius, Virgo, Libra, Aquarius, Capricorn, Scorpio, Pisces 0; any other answer 2.)

A subtle question. Astrology is nonsense. He hated people who asked him what sign he was (his stock reply was 'My sign? No entry') and he was on the lookout for people with a similar view. He didn't mind people reading their horoscopes in magazines etc, but he didn't think he could bear to live with anyone who took it seriously.

> 10a. Wine, beer or other (if other please specify)? (Neither/vodka/bacardi 0, gin 1, wine 2, beer 2.)

This led on to a complicated set of sub questions:

If wine

> 10b Red or white?
> (White 0, red 1.)

Being as reactionary as his father, he was of the old fashioned school that there is no such thing as white wine. Unlike his father, he actually drank it.

If red

> 10c chilled?
> (Yes 0, no 1.)

If beer

> **10b beer or lager?**
> (lager 0, beer 1)

If beer

> **10c pint or half?**
> (pint 1, half 1/2)

He loved women who drank pints, but recognised that there was sometimes a need for moderation, especially given what he'd read about their different metabolisms.

He had his misgivings about question ten. It was complicated and he was worried that it made it seem as though alcohol had an overweening importance in his life. But then he reasoned that, well, alcohol did have an overweening importance in his life. And he really couldn't live with a tee-totaller, could he? His parents had forbidden the demon drink from the house, and there had been so many disagreements about it when he'd started experimenting. Besides, choice of drink said crucial things about a person. He felt, for instance, much the same about Bacardi drinkers as he did about people who read the Daily Mail: viz that they lived in another universe. Vodka was (in Scotland at least) alcohol for people who didn't really like alcohol, and it led to that ultimate in barbarism, the vodka and Irn Bru.

> **11 Should Scotland be independent?**
> (No 0, Yes 2.)

He was thinking of dropping this question in favour of something more penetrating. Almost everyone had got it right, even the English girls who'd done

119

the questionnaire. Everyone thought that Scotland should be independent, just as no-one thought that it ever would be.·

---

12 Have you ever been to Butlins?
(Yes (unqualified) 0, No 1, Yes (as a child) 2.)

There was a tricky balance to be achieved here between, on the one hand, the limited horizons which some choices of holiday destination said about a person, and, on the other hand, that touch of gritty proletarian realism which childhood sojourns in holiday camps spoke of. He himself had spent many a miserable week in a chalet in October. The family went away at half term, when it was cheaper. The cold was character building. If he could find a girl with similar experiences he knew he would be on to a good thing though he would have to make sure that she did not share his own depressive tendencies. This was the reason for question 13.

---

13 The universe is a lonely, bleak and barren place, devoid of meaning and solace, and man (and woman) is an insignificant speck in this void. Do you agree?
(No 0, yes 1, up to a point/sort of etc 2.)

Answering 'no' to this question spoke, in his view, of a lack of depth and vision. Answering 'yes' was preferable, though it did open up the possibility of a dark streak running through the respondent's personality. This could, of course, make a person interesting, but there was also the danger of her reminding him too much of his father. It was something which would have to be weighed up against the other responses.

This was primarily a way of weeding out the Edinburgh parochials. It was funny but you just knew that if a person answered 'salt and sauce' to this question, then Edinburgh, the only place in the universe where salt and sauce was available in the fish supper context, was the be-all and end-all of their universe. It had nothing to do with his Glaswegian origins. He wanted someone with the broader horizons that the use of vinegar implied. The use of tomato ketchup he considered barbaric, and was one of his criteria for sudden death elimination.

He didn't think he could bear to live with a Christian, though he was almost willing to consider certain varieties of Catholic (lapsed). He wondered about Buddhists, Hindus and Sikhs, though none had ever attempted the questionnaire. He expected they'd be just as tiresome in the end, and would want him to go to their equivalent of kirk on their equivalent of Sunday morning, so he thought he'd give them a wide berth anyway.

His own relations with his parents were amicable. He rarely saw them, of course, which helped, and he certainly got on with them now a great deal better than he had when he'd lived with them. They still disapproved of his godlessness and his leftish political views, though these were things they expected him to grow out of. He'd met girls whose parents were forever popping round for cups of coffee or going out shopping with them. His own experience and theirs seemed to him to be separated by such a yawning chasm that he would never be able to get on with them. By the same token, he'd met girls who had dyed their hair orange at fourteen and started smoking in the house to rebel. He'd never found the courage to do that, but he did at least have the self-knowledge to realise that a woman who could do that at fourteen would very probably walk all over him now.

17. On top or underneath?

Another of the 'open' questions. He didn't specify an answer, awarding marks for interpretation and applicability. Many of the respondents thought (correctly) that this question was sexual, and answered according to their own tastes. Others thought it was sexual and answered according to what, not knowing of his lack of actual experience, they guessed of his ('you underneath', 2 points). The girl who'd got the Celtic or

18. Where do you see yourself in five years time?

This particular open question was one which he'd been asked at every job interview he ever attended. He was longing to find out what the correct answer was.

19a Television is killing off the art of conversation. Agree or disagree?
(Disagree 0, maybe 1, agree 2)

The answer to this one was patently obvious. He knew just how many people spent their entire leisure time sitting and staring at the TV set. It was surprising, though, how many people had no idea. The question was there to winnow out the couch potatoes. It had a supplement:

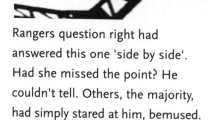

Rangers question right had answered this one 'side by side'. Had she missed the point? He couldn't tell. Others, the majority, had simply stared at him, bemused.

19b Favourite television programme

He could permit a girl one or two favourite programmes, but that was all. Anyone who listed more than two was out. Anyone who mentioned Brookside or Coronation Street was out. Anyone who mentioned anything on ITV apart from the South Bank Show was out. Newsnight or Panorama scored 2 points.

20 Spell and define the word 'mnemonic'.

The one truly elitist question on the list, apart from, if he was honest with himself, 1, 5, 10, 12, 14 and 19a and 19b. He hated to admit it, but he was a bit of a snob. He'd reasoned that someone who knew this word would be more capable of conversation than his mother. Not that that was saying much.

He'd had 103 responses, but no scores in the nineties, let alone the perfect 100. One at 86%. Three years ago now. He'd even called the 86% girl, Jenny, the other day, but she was going out with someone else.

Just recently, he'd been starting to wonder whether he was being a bit too pernickety. He was getting on a bit, though his mother had said that a man is still very attractive in his mid-thirties. But then, she'd been the one who'd told him that one day the ideal girl would come along. He was beginning to question her judgement. He'd started wondering whether he would die a virgin. Actually, now, sitting there and thinking about it really hard, he was beginning to ask himself all sorts of questions.

come

This first novel by club promoter
and multimedia terrorist Mark
Waugh is an original mix of
narrative, anti-narrative and BPM
(Beyond Post Modernist)
philosophy.

   Dolly Savage is an inflatable
doll who becomes a cult movie
star and international icon of cool.
Her career is observed by
Marks 0 and 1, one of whom steals
the disc containing the other's
novel, remixes and publishes it.

Mark Waugh

Limited edition
including CD mini-
album available
from selected
shops

A writer to watch out for.
Evening Standard

Imagine a George Romero
zombie-flick remixed by
Luis Bunuel on a bad day
at Eurodisney.
Steve Beard, i-D

A bilious critique of
haywire consumerism and
corporate hypocrisy laced
with 90's cultural
atrophy. Repulsive,
engrossing and hilarious.
Book of the month.
G-SPOT

their
HEADS
are
anonymous

Alistair Gentry

A novel about desire, secret histories
and psychic insects

rice
new black fiction
peas

Edited by Patsy Antoine, this collection showcases original fiction by the new generation of black British authors.

Open to writers/artists of African, Asian, Carribbean and mixed-race origins. Send typescripts (from 500-5,000 words) to:

Patsy Antoine, New Nation, Gateway House, Milverton Street, London SE11 4AP. Absolutely no telephone queries.

Submissions deadline: 1/9/97.

Mail Order

I enclose a cheque payable to *PULP Faction* for:

- ☐ £8.99 THEIR HEADS ARE ANONYMOUS   *Alistair Gentry*
- ☐ £8.99 COME (book only)   *Mark Waugh*
- ☐ £7.99 CALL ME   *P-P Hartnett*

- ☐ £18.00 Any 3 of the following titles (please specify):
  - ☐ £5.99 SKIN
  - ☐ £6.99 TECHNOPAGAN
  - ☐ £6.99 THE LIVING ROOM
  - ☐ £6.99 FISSION
  - ☐ £6.99 RANDOM FACTOR
  - ☐ £7.50 ALLNIGHTER
  - ☐ £7.50 5 UNEASY PIECES

- ☐ Please include submission details for future titles.

Name ....

Address ....

....

Postcode ....

Return to: Pulp Faction, BooksDirect, PO Box 12171, London, N19 3HB.
Books delivered post-free to any UK address within 28 days.
Orders from outside the UK, add £1.50 p&p per book or £4 per multibuy.